Nathaniel Hawthorne (July 4, 1804 – May 19, 1864) was an American novelist, dark romantic, and short story writer. His works often focus on history, morality, and religion. He was born in 1804 in Salem, Massachusetts, to Nathaniel Hathorne and the former Elizabeth Clarke Manning. His ancestors include John Hathorne, the only judge involved in the Salem witch trials who never repented of his actions. He entered Bowdoin College in 1821, was elected to Phi Beta Kappa in 1824, and graduated in 1825. He published his first work in 1828, the novel Fanshawe; he later tried to suppress it, feeling that it was not equal to the standard of his later work. He published several short stories in periodicals, which he collected in 1837 as Twice-Told Tales. The next year, he became engaged to Sophia Peabody. He worked at the Boston Custom House and joined Brook Farm, a transcendentalist community, before marrying Peabody in 1842. The couple moved to The Old Manse in Concord, Massachusetts, later moving to Salem, the Berkshires, then to The Wayside in Concord. (Source: Wikipedia)

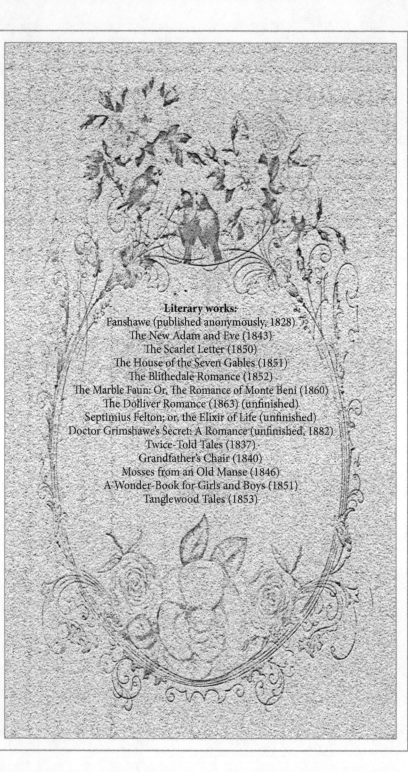

Literary works:
Fanshawe (published anonymously, 1828)
The New Adam and Eve (1843)
The Scarlet Letter (1850)
The House of the Seven Gables (1851)
The Blithedale Romance (1852)
The Marble Faun: Or, The Romance of Monte Beni (1860)
The Dolliver Romance (1863) (unfinished)
Septimius Felton; or, the Elixir of Life (unfinished)
Doctor Grimshawe's Secret: A Romance (unfinished, 1882)
Twice-Told Tales (1837)
Grandfather's Chair (1840)
Mosses from an Old Manse (1846)
A Wonder-Book for Girls and Boys (1851)
Tanglewood Tales (1853)

THE ANCESTRAL FOOTSTEP
OUTLINES OF AN ENGLISH ROMANCE
NATHANIEL HAWTHORNE

PRINCE CLASSICS

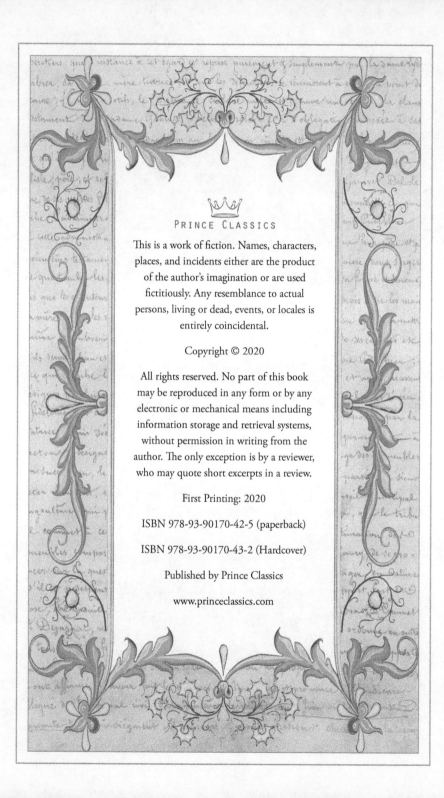

PRINCE CLASSICS

First Printing: 2020

ISBN 978-93-90170-42-5 (paperback)

ISBN 978-93-90170-43-2 (Hardcover)

Published by Prince Classics

www.princeclassics.com

Contents

INTRODUCTORY NOTE.   9

I.   13

II.   36

III.   61

About Author   87

NOTABLE WORKS   99

THE ANCESTRAL FOOTSTEP
OUTLINES OF AN ENGLISH ROMANCE

INTRODUCTORY NOTE.

"Septimius Felton" was the outgrowth of a project, formed by Hawthorne during his residence in England, of writing a romance, the scene of which should be laid in that country; but this project was afterwards abandoned, giving place to a new conception in which the visionary search for means to secure an earthly immortality was to form the principal interest. The new conception took shape in the uncompleted "Dolliver Romance." The two themes, of course, were distinct, but, by a curious process of thought, one grew directly out of the other: the whole history constitutes, in fact, a chapter in what may be called the genealogy of a romance. There remained, after "Septimius Felton" had been published, certain manuscripts connected with the scheme of an English story. One of these manuscripts was written in the form of a journalized narrative; the author merely noting the date of what he wrote, as he went along. The other was a more extended sketch, of much greater bulk, and without date, but probably produced several years later. It was not originally intended by those who at the time had charge of Hawthorne's papers that either of these incomplete writings should be laid before the public; because they manifestly had not been left by him in a form which he would have considered as warranting such a course. But since the second and larger manuscript has been published under the title of "Dr. Grimshawe's Secret," it has been thought best to issue the present sketch, so that the two documents may be examined together. Their appearance places in the hands of readers the entire process of development leading to the "Septimius" and "The Dolliver Romance." They speak for themselves much more efficiently than any commentator can expect to do; and little, therefore, remains to be said beyond a few words of explanation in regard to the following pages.

The Note-Books show that the plan of an English romance, turning upon the fact that an emigrant to America had carried away a family secret which should give his descendant the power to ruin the family in the mother country, had occurred to Hawthorne as early as April, 1855. In August of the same year he visited Smithell's Hall, in Bolton le Moors, concerning which he had already heard its legend of "The Bloody Footstep," and from that time on, the idea of this footprint on the threshold-stone of the ancestral mansion seems to have associated itself inextricably with the dreamy substance of his yet unshaped romance. Indeed, it leaves its mark broadly upon Sibyl Dacy's wild legend in "Septimius Felton," and reappears in the last paragraph of that story. But, so far as we can know at this day, nothing definite was done until after his departure for Italy. It was then, while staying in Rome, that he began to put upon paper that plot which had first occupied his thoughts three years before, in the scant leisure allowed him by his duties at the Liverpool consulate. Of leisure there was not a great deal at Rome, either; for, as the "French and Italian Note-Books" show, sight-seeing and social intercourse took up a good deal of his time, and the daily record in his journal likewise had to be kept up. But he set to work resolutely to embody, so far as he might, his stray imaginings upon the haunting English theme, and to give them connected form. April 1, 1858, he began; and then nearly two weeks passed before he found an opportunity to resume; April 13th being the date of the next passage. By May he gets fully into swing, so that day after day, with but slight breaks, he carries on the story, always increasing in interest for us who read as for him who improvised. Thus it continues until May 19th, by which time he has made a tolerably complete outline, filled in with a good deal of detail here and there. Although the sketch is cast in the form of a regular narrative, one or two gaps occur, indicating that the author had thought out certain points which he then took for granted without making note of them. Brief scenes, passages of conversation and of narration, follow one another after the manner of a finished story, alternating with synopses of the plot, and queries concerning particulars that needed further study; confidences of the romancer to himself which form certainly a valuable contribution to literary history. The manuscript closes with a rapid sketch of the conclusion, and the way in which it is to be executed. Succinctly, what we have here is a romance in embryo; one, moreover, that never attained to a viable stature and constitution. During his lifetime it naturally would not have been put forward as demanding public attention; and, in consideration of that fact, it has since been withheld from the press by the decision of his daughter, in whom the title to it vests. Students of literary art, however, and many more general readers will, I think, be likely to discover in it a charm all the greater for its being in parts only indicated; since, as it stands, it presents the precise condition of a work of fiction in its first stage. The unfinished "Grimshawe" was another development of the same theme, and the "Septimius" a later sketch, with a new element introduced. But the present experimental fragment, to which it has been decided to give the title of "The Ancestral Footstep," possesses a freshness and spontaneity recalling the peculiar fascination of those chalk or pencil outlines with which great masters in the graphic art have been wont to arrest their fleeting glimpses of a composition still unwrought.

It would not be safe to conclude, from the large amount of preliminary writing done with a view to that romance, that Hawthorne always adopted this laborious mode of making several drafts of a book. On the contrary, it is understood that his habit was to mature a design so thoroughly in his mind before attempting to give it actual existence on paper that but little rewriting was needed. The circumstance that he was obliged to write so much that did not satisfy him in this case may account partly for his relinquishing the theme, as one which for him had lost its seductiveness through too much recasting.

It need be added only that the original manuscript, from which the following pages are printed through the medium of an exact copy, is singularly clear and fluent. Not a single correction occurs throughout; but here and there a word is omitted, obviously by mere accident, and these omissions have been supplied. The correction in each case is marked by brackets, in this printed reproduction. The sketch begins abruptly; but there is no reason to suppose that anything preceded it except the unrecorded musings in the author's mind, and one or two memoranda in the "English Note-Books." We must therefore imagine the central figure, Middleton, who is the American descendant of an old English family, as having been properly introduced, and then pass at once to the opening sentences. The rest will explain itself.

G. P. L.

I.

April 1, 1858. *Thursday.*—He had now been travelling long in those rich portions of England where he would most have wished to find the object of his pursuit; and many had been the scenes which he would willingly have identified with that mentioned in the ancient, time-yellowed record which he bore about with him. It is to be observed that, undertaken at first half as the amusement, the unreal object, of a grown man's play-day, it had become more and more real to him with every step of the way that he followed it up; along those green English lanes it seemed as if everything would bring him close to the mansion that he sought; every morning he went on with renewed hopes, nor did the evening, though it brought with it no success, bring with it the gloom and heaviness of a real disappointment. In all his life, including its earliest and happiest days, he had never known such a spring and zest as now filled his veins, and gave lightsomeness to his limbs; this spirit gave to the beautiful country which he trod a still richer beauty than it had ever borne, and he sought his ancient home as if he had found his way into Paradise and were there endeavoring to trace out the sight [site] of Eve's bridal bower, the birthplace of the human race and its glorious possibilities of happiness and high performance.

In these sweet and delightful moods of mind, varying from one dream to another, he loved indeed the solitude of his way; but likewise he loved the facility which his pursuit afforded him, of coming in contact with many varieties of men, and he took advantage of this facility to an extent which it was not usually his impulse to do. But now he came forth from all reserves, and offered himself to whomever the chances of the way offered to him, with a ready sensibility that made its way through every barrier that even English exclusiveness, in whatever rank of life, could set up. The plastic character of Middleton was perhaps a variety of American nature only presenting itself under an individual form; he could throw off the man of our day, and put on a ruder nature, but then it was with a certain fineness, that made this only [a] distinction between it and the central truth. He found less variety of form in the English character than he had been accustomed to see at home; but perhaps this was in consequence of the external nature of his acquaintance with it; for the view of one well accustomed to a people, and of a stranger to them, differs in this—that the latter sees the homogeneity, the one universal character, the groundwork of the whole, while the former sees a thousand little differences, which distinguish the individual men apart, to such a degree that they seem hardly to have any resemblance among themselves.

But just at the period of his journey when we take him up, Middleton had been for two or three days the companion of an old man who interested him more than most of his wayside companions; the more especially as he seemed to be wandering without an object, or with such a dreamy object as that which led Middleton's own steps onward. He was a plain old man enough, but with a pale, strong-featured face and white hair, a certain picturesqueness and venerableness, which Middleton fancied might have befitted a richer garb than he now wore. In much of their conversation, too, he was sensible that, though the stranger betrayed no acquaintance with literature, nor seemed to have conversed with cultivated minds, yet the results of such acquaintance and converse were here. Middleton was inclined to think him, however, an old man, one of those itinerants, such as Wordsworth represented in the "Excursion," who smooth themselves by the attrition of the world and gain a knowledge equivalent to or better than that of books from the actual intellect of man awake and active around them.

Often, during the short period since their companionship originated, Middleton had felt impelled to disclose to the old man the object of his journey, and the wild tale by which, after two hundred years, he had been blown as it were across the ocean, and drawn onward to commence this search. The old man's ordinary conversation was of a nature to draw forth such a confidence as this; frequently turning on the traditions of the wayside; the reminiscences that lingered on the battle-fields of the Roses, or of the Parliament, like flowers nurtured by the blood of the slain, and prolonging their race through the centuries for the wayfarer to pluck them; or the family histories of the castles, manor-houses, and seats which, of various epochs, had their park-gates along the roadside and would be seen with dark gray towers or ancient gables, or more modern forms of architecture, rising up among clouds of ancient oaks. Middleton watched earnestly to see if, in any of these tales, there were circumstances resembling those striking and singular ones which he had borne so long in his memory, and on which he was now acting in so strange a manner; but [though] there was a good deal of variety of incident in them, there never was any combination of incidents having the peculiarity of this.

"I suppose," said he to the old man, "the settlers in my country may have carried away with them traditions long since forgotten in this country, but which might have an interest and connection, and might even piece out the broken relics of family history, which have remained perhaps a mystery for hundreds of years. I can conceive, even, that this might be of importance in settling the heirships of estates; but which now, only the two insulated parts of the story being known, remain a riddle, although the solution of it is actually in the world, if only these two parts could be united across the sea, like the wires of an electric telegraph."

"It is an impressive idea," said the old man. "Do you know any such tradition as you have hinted at?"

April 13th.—Middleton could not but wonder at the singular chance that had established him in such a place, and in such society, so strangely adapted to the purposes with which he had been wandering through England. He had come hither, hoping as it were to find the past still alive and in action; and here it was so in this one only spot, and these few persons into the midst of whom he had suddenly been cast. With these reflections he looked forth from his window into the old-fashioned garden, and at the stone sundial, which had numbered all the hours—all the daylight and serene ones, at least—since his mysterious ancestor left the country. And [is] this, then, he thought to himself, the establishment of which some rumor had been preserved? Was it here that the secret had its hiding-place in the old coffer, in the cupboard, in the secret chamber, or whatever was indicated by the apparently idle words of the document which he had preserved? He still smiled at the idea, but it was with a pleasant, mysterious sense that his life had at last got out of the dusty real, and that strangeness had mixed itself up with his daily experience.

15

With such feelings he prepared himself to go down to dinner with his host. He found him alone at table, which was placed in a dark old room modernized with every English comfort and the pleasant spectacle of a table set with the whitest of napery and the brightest of glass and china. The friendly old gentleman, as he had found him from the first, became doubly and trebly so in that position which brings out whatever warmth of heart an Englishman has, and gives it to him if he has none. The impressionable and sympathetic character of Middleton answered to the kindness of his host; and by the time the meal was concluded, the two were conversing with almost as much zest and friendship as if they were similar in age, even fellow-countrymen, and had known one another all their life-time. Middleton's secret, it may be supposed, came often to the tip of his tongue; but still he kept it within, from a natural repugnance to bring out the one romance of his life. The talk, however, necessarily ran much upon topics among which this one would have come in without any extra attempt to introduce it.

"This decay of old families," said the Master, "is much greater than would appear on the surface of things. We have such a reluctance to part with them, that we are content to see them continued by any fiction, through any indirections, rather than to dispense with old names. In your country, I suppose, there is no such reluctance; you are willing that one generation should blot out all that preceded it, and be itself the newest and only age of the world."

"Not quite so," answered Middleton; "at any rate, if there be such a feeling in the people at large, I doubt whether, even in England, those who fancy themselves possessed of claims to birth, cherish them more as a treasure than we do. It is, of course, a thousand times more difficult for us to keep alive a name amid a thousand difficulties sedulously thrown around it by our institutions, than for you to do, where your institutions are anxiously calculated to promote the contrary purpose. It has occasionally struck me, however, that the ancient lineage might often be found in America, for a family which has been compelled to prolong itself here through the female line, and through alien stocks."

16

"Indeed, my young friend," said the Master, "if that be the case, I should like to [speak?] further with you upon it; for, I can assure you, there are sometimes vicissitudes in old families that make me grieve to think that a man cannot be made for the occasion."

All this while, the young lady at table had remained almost silent; and Middleton had only occasionally been reminded of her by the necessity of performing some of those offices which put people at table under a Christian necessity of recognizing one another. He was, to say the truth, somewhat interested in her, yet not strongly attracted by the neutral tint of her dress, and the neutral character of her manners. She did not seem to be handsome, although, with her face full before him, he had not quite made up his mind on this point.

April 14th.—So here was Middleton, now at length seeing indistinctly a thread, to which the thread that he had so long held in his hand—the hereditary thread that ancestor after ancestor had handed down—might seem ready to join on. He felt as if they were the two points of an electric chain, which being joined, an instantaneous effect must follow. Earnestly, as he would have looked forward to this moment (had he in sober reason ever put any real weight on the fantasy in pursuit of which he had wandered so far) he now, that it actually appeared to be realizing itself, paused with a vague sensation of alarm. The mystery was evidently one of sorrow, if not of crime, and he felt as if that sorrow and crime might not have been annihilated even by being buried out of human sight and remembrance so long. He remembered to have heard or read, how that once an old pit had been dug open, in which were found the remains of persons that, as the shuddering by-standers traditionally remembered, had died of an ancient pestilence; and out of that old grave had come a new plague, that slew the far-off progeny of those who had first died by it. Might not some fatal treasure like this, in a moral view, be brought to light by the secret into which he had so strangely been drawn? Such were the fantasies with which he awaited the return of Alice, whose light footsteps sounded afar along the passages of the old mansion; and then all was silent.

At length he heard the sound, a great way off, as he concluded, of her returning footstep, approaching from chamber to chamber, and along the staircases, closing the doors behind her. At first, he paid no great attention to the character of these sounds, but as they drew nearer, he became aware that the footstep was unlike those of Alice; indeed, as unlike as could be, very regular, slow, yet not firm, so that it seemed to be that of an aged person, sauntering listlessly through the rooms. We have often alluded to Middleton's sensitiveness, and the quick vibrations of his sympathies; and there was something in this slow approach that produced a strange feeling within him; so that he stood breathlessly, looking towards the door by which these slow footsteps were to enter. At last, there appeared in the doorway a venerable figure, clad in a rich, faded dressing-gown, and standing on the threshold looked fixedly at Middleton, at the same time holding up a light in his left hand. In his right was some object that Middleton did not distinctly see. But he knew the figure, and recognized the face. It was the old man, his long since companion on the journey hitherward.

"So," said the old man, smiling gravely, "you have thought fit, at last, to accept the hospitality which I offered you so long ago. It might have been better for both of us—for all parties—if you had accepted it then!"

"You here!" exclaimed Middleton. "And what can be your connection with all the error and trouble, and involuntary wrong, through which I have wandered since our last meeting? And is it possible that you even then held the clue which I was seeking?"

"No,—no," replied Rothermel. "I was not conscious, at least, of so doing. And yet had we two sat down there by the wayside, or on that English stile, which attracted your attention so much; had we sat down there and thrown forth each his own dream, each his own knowledge, it would have saved much that we must now forever regret. Are you even now ready to confide wholly in me?"

"Alas," said Middleton, with a darkening brow, "there are many reasons, at this moment, which did not exist then, to incline me to hold my peace. And why has not Alice returned?—and what is your connection with her?"

"Let her answer for herself," said Rothermel; and he called her, shouting through the silent house as if she were at the furthest chamber, and he were in instant need: "Alice!—Alice!—Alice!—here is one who would know what is the link between a maiden and her father!"

Amid the strange uproar which he made Alice came flying back, not in alarm but only in haste, and put her hand within his own. "Hush, father," said she. "It is not time."

Here is an abstract of the plot of this story. The Middleton who emigrated to America, more than two hundred years ago, had been a dark and moody man; he came with a beautiful though not young woman for his wife, and left a family behind him. In this family a certain heirloom had been preserved, and with it a tradition that grew wilder and stranger with the passing generations. The tradition had lost, if it ever had, some of its connecting links; but it referred to a murder, to the expulsion of a brother from the hereditary house, in some strange way, and to a Bloody Footstep which he had left impressed into the threshold, as he turned about to make a last remonstrance. It was rumored, however, or vaguely understood, that the expelled brother was not altogether an innocent man; but that there had been wrong done, as well as crime committed, insomuch that his reasons were strong that led him, subsequently, to imbibe the most gloomy religious views, and to bury himself in the Western wilderness. These reasons he had never fully imparted to his family; but had necessarily made allusions to them, which had been treasured up and doubtless enlarged upon. At last, one descendant of the family determines to go to England, with the purpose of searching out whatever ground there may be for these traditions, carrying with him certain ancient documents, and other relics; and goes about the country, half in earnest, and half in sport of fancy, in quest of the old family mansion. He makes singular discoveries, all of which bring the book to an end unexpected by everybody, and not satisfactory to the natural yearnings of novel readers. In the traditions that he brought over, there was a key to some family secrets that were still unsolved, and that controlled the descent of estates and titles. His influence upon these matters involves [him] in divers strange and perilous adventures; and at last it turns out that he himself is the rightful heir to the titles and estate, that had passed into another name within the last half-century. But he respects both, feeling that it is better to make a virgin soil than to try to make the old name grow in a soil that had been darkened with so much blood and misfortune as this.

April 27th. Tuesday.—It was with a delightful feeling of release from ordinary rules, that Middleton found himself brought into this connection with Alice; and he only hoped that this play-day of his life might last long enough to rest him from all that he had suffered. In the enjoyment of his position he almost forgot the pursuit that occupied him, nor might he have remembered for a long space if, one evening, Alice herself had not alluded to it. "You are wasting precious days," she suddenly said. "Why do not you renew your quest?"

"To what do you allude?" said Middleton, in surprise. "What object do you suppose me to have?"

Alice smiled; nay, laughed outright. "You suppose yourself to be a perfect mystery, no doubt," she replied. "But do not I know you—have not I known you long—as the holder of the talisman, the owner of the mysterious cabinet that contains the blood-stained secret?"

"Nay, Alice, this is certainly a strange coincidence, that you should know even thus much of a foolish secret that makes me employ this little holiday time, which I have stolen out of a weary life, in a wild-goose chase. But, believe me, you allude to matters that are more a mystery to me than my affairs appear to be to you. Will you explain what you would suggest by this badinage?"

Alice shook her head. "You have no claim to know what I know, even if it would be any addition to your own knowledge. I shall not, and must not enlighten you. You must burrow for the secret with your own tools, in your own manner, and in a place of your own choosing. I am bound not to assist you."

"Alice, this is wilful, wayward, unjust," cried Middleton, with a flushed cheek. "I have not told you—yet you know well—the deep and real importance which this subject has for me. We have been together as friends, yet, the instant when there comes up an occasion when the slightest friendly feeling would induce you to do me a good office, you assume this altered tone."

"My tone is not in the least altered in respect to you," said Alice. "All along, as you know, I have reserved myself on this very point; it being, I candidly tell you, impossible for me to act in your interest in the matter alluded to. If you choose to consider this unfriendly, as being less than the terms on which you conceive us to have stood give you a right to demand of me—you must resent it as you please. I shall not the less retain for you the regard due to one who has certainly befriended me in very untoward circumstances."

This conversation confirmed the previous idea of Middleton, that some mystery of a peculiarly dark and evil character was connected with the family secret with which he was himself entangled; but it perplexed him to imagine in what way this, after the lapse of so many years, should continue to be a matter of real importance at the present day. All the actors in the original guilt—if guilt it were—must have been long ago in their graves; some in the churchyard of the village, with those moss-grown letters embossing their names; some in the church itself, with mural tablets recording their names over the family-pew, and one, it might be, far over the sea, where his grave was first made under the forest leaves, though now a city had grown up around it. Yet here was he, the remote descendant of that family, setting his foot at last in the country, and as secretly as might be; and all at once his mere presence seemed to revive the buried secret, almost to awake the dead who partook of that secret and had acted it. There was a vibration from the other world, continued and prolonged into this, the instant that he stepped upon the mysterious and haunted ground.

He knew not in what way to proceed. He could not but feel that there was something not exactly within the limits of propriety in being here, disguised—at least, not known in his true character—prying into the secrets of a proud and secluded Englishman. But then, as he said to himself on his own side of the question, the secret belonged to himself by exactly as ancient a tenure and by precisely as strong a claim, as to the Englishman. His rights here were just as powerful and well-founded as those of his ancestor had been, nearly three centuries ago; and here the same feeling came over him that he was that very personage, returned after all these ages, to see if his foot would fit this bloody footstep left of old upon the threshold. The result of all his cogitation was, as the reader will have foreseen, that he decided to continue his researches, and, his proceedings being pretty defensible, let the result take care of itself.

For this purpose he went next day to the hospital, and ringing at the Master's door, was ushered into the old-fashioned, comfortable library, where he had spent that well-remembered evening which threw the first ray of light on the pursuit that now seemed developing into such strange and unexpected consequences. Being admitted, he was desired by the domestic to wait, as his Reverence was at that moment engaged with a gentleman on business. Glancing through the ivy that mantled over the window, Middleton saw that this interview was taking place in the garden, where the Master and his visitor were walking to and fro in the avenue of box, discussing some matter, as it seemed to him, with considerable earnestness on both sides. He observed, too, that there was warmth, passion, a disturbed feeling on the stranger's part; while, on that of the Master, it was a calm, serious, earnest representation of whatever view he was endeavoring to impress on the other. At last, the interview appeared to come toward a climax, the Master addressing some words to his guest, still with undisturbed calmness, to which the latter replied by a violent and even fierce gesture, as it should seem of menace, not towards the Master, but some unknown party; and then hastily turning, he left the garden and was soon heard riding away. The Master looked after him awhile, and then, shaking his white head, returned into the house and soon entered the parlor.

He looked somewhat surprised, and, as it struck Middleton, a little startled, at finding him there; yet he welcomed him with all his former cordiality—indeed, with a friendship that thoroughly warmed Middleton's heart even to its coldest corner.

"This is strange!" said the old gentleman. "Do you remember our conversation on that evening when I first had the unlooked-for pleasure of receiving you as a guest into my house? At that time I spoke to you of a strange family story, of which there was no denouement, such as a novel-writer would desire, and which had remained in that unfinished posture for more than two hundred years! Well; perhaps it will gratify you to know that there seems a prospect of that wanting termination being supplied!"

"Indeed!" said Middleton.

"Yes," replied the Master. "A gentleman has just parted with me who was indeed the representative of the family concerned in the story. He is the descendant of a younger son of that family, to whom the estate devolved about a century ago, although at that time there was search for the heirs of the elder son, who had disappeared after the bloody incident which I related to you. Now, singular as it may appear, at this late day, a person claiming to be the descendant and heir of that eldest son has appeared, and if I may credit my friend's account, is disposed not only to claim the estate, but the dormant title which Eldredge himself has been so long preparing to claim for himself. Singularly enough, too, the heir is an American."

May 2d, Sunday.—"I believe," said Middleton, "that many English secrets might find their solution in America, if the two threads of a story could be brought together, disjoined as they have been by time and the ocean. But are you at liberty to tell me the nature of the incidents to which you allude?"

"I do not see any reason to the contrary," answered the Master; "for the story has already come in an imperfect way before the public, and the full and authentic particulars are likely soon to follow. It seems that the younger brother was ejected from the house on account of a love affair; the elder having married a young woman with whom the younger was in love, and, it is said, the wife disappeared on the bridal night, and was never heard of more. The elder brother remained single during the rest of his life; and dying childless, and there being still no news of the second brother, the inheritance and representation of the family devolved upon the third brother and his posterity. This branch of the family has ever since remained in possession; and latterly the representation has become of more importance, on account of a claim to an old title, which, by the failure of another branch of this ancient family, has devolved upon the branch here settled. Now, just at this juncture, comes another heir from America, pretending that he is the descendant of a marriage between the second son, supposed to have been murdered on the threshold of the manor-house, and the missing bride! Is it not a singular story?"

"It would seem to require very strong evidence to prove it," said Middleton. "And methinks a Republican should care little for the title, however he might value the estate."

"Both—both," said the Master, smiling, "would be equally attractive to your countryman. But there are further curious particulars in connection with this claim. You must know, they are a family of singular characteristics, humorists, sometimes developing their queer traits into something like insanity; though oftener, I must say, spending stupid hereditary lives here on their estates, rusting out and dying without leaving any biography whatever about them. And yet there has always been one very queer thing about this generally very commonplace family. It is that each father, on his death-bed, has had an interview with his son, at which he has imparted some secret that has evidently had an influence on the character and after life of the son, making him ever after a discontented man, aspiring for something he has never been able to find. Now the American, I am told, pretends that he has the clue which has always been needed to make the secret available; the key whereby the lock may be opened; the something that the lost son of the family carried away with him, and by which through these centuries he has impeded the progress of the race. And, wild as the story seems, he does certainly seem to bring something that looks very like the proof of what he says."

"And what are those proofs?" inquired Middleton, wonder-stricken at the strange reduplication of his own position and pursuits.

"In the first place," said the Master, "the English marriage-certificate by a clergyman of that day in London, after publication of the banns, with a reference to the register of the parish church where the marriage is recorded. Then, a certified genealogy of the family in New England, where such matters can be ascertained from town and church records, with at least as much certainty, it would appear, as in this country. He has likewise a manuscript in his ancestor's autograph, containing a brief account of the events which banished him from his own country; the circumstances which favored the idea that he had been slain, and which he himself was willing should be received as a belief; the fortune that led him to America, where he wished to found a new race wholly disconnected with the past; and this manuscript he sealed up, with directions that it should not be opened till two hundred years after his death, by which time, as it was probable to conjecture, it would matter little to any mortal whether the story was told or not. A whole generation has passed since the time when the paper was at last unsealed and read, so long it had no operation; yet now, at last, here comes the American, to disturb the succession of an ancient family!"

"There is something very strange in all this," said Middleton.

And indeed there was something stranger in his view of the matter than he had yet communicated to the Master. For, taking into consideration the relation in which he found himself with the present recognized representative of the family, the thought struck him that his coming hither had dug up, as it were, a buried secret that immediately assumed life and activity the moment that it was above ground again. For seven generations the family had vegetated in the quietude of English country gentility, doing nothing to make itself known, passing from the cradle to the tomb amid the same old woods that had waved over it before his ancestor had impressed the bloody footstep; and yet the instant that he came back, an influence seemed to be at work that was likely to renew the old history of the family. He questioned with himself whether it were not better to leave all as it was; to withdraw himself into the secrecy from which he had but half emerged, and leave the family to keep on, to the end of time perhaps, in its rusty innocence, rather than to interfere with his wild American character to disturb it. The smell of that dark crime—that brotherly hatred and attempted murder—seemed to breathe out of the ground as he dug it up. Was it not better that it should remain forever buried, for what to him was this old English title—what this estate, so far from his own native land, located amidst feelings and manners which would never be his own? It was late, to be sure—yet not too late for him to turn back: the vibration, the fear, which his footsteps had caused, would subside into peace! Meditating in this way, he took a hasty leave of the kind old Master, promising to see him again at an early opportunity. By chance, or however it was, his footsteps turned to the woods of —— Chace, and there he wandered through its glades, deep in thought, yet always with a strange sense that he was treading on the soil where his ancestors had trodden, and where he himself had best right of all men to be. It was just in this state of feeling that he found his course arrested by a hand upon his shoulder.

"What business have you here?" was the question sounded in his ear; and, starting, he found himself in the grasp, as his blood tingled to know, of a gentleman in a shooting-dress, who looked at him with a wrathful brow. "Are you a poacher, or what?"

Be the case what it might, Middleton's blood boiled at the grasp of that hand, as it never before had done in the course of his impulsive life. He shook himself free, and stood fiercely before his antagonist, confronting him with his uplifted stick, while the other, likewise, appeared to be shaken by a strange wrath.

"Fellow," muttered he—"Yankee blackguard!—impostor—take yourself oil these grounds. Quick, or it will be the worse for you!"

Middleton restrained himself. "Mr. Eldredge," said he, "for I believe I speak to the man who calls himself owner of this land on which we stand,— Mr. Eldredge, you are acting under a strange misapprehension of my character. I have come hither with no sinister purpose, and am entitled, at the hands of a gentleman, to the consideration of an honorable antagonist, even if you deem me one at all. And perhaps, if you think upon the blue chamber and the ebony cabinet, and the secret connected with it,"—

"Villain, no more!" said Eldredge; and utterly mad with rage, he presented his gun at Middleton; but even at the moment of doing so, he partly restrained himself, so far as, instead of shooting him, to raise the butt of his gun, and strike a blow at him. It came down heavily on Middleton's shoulder, though aimed at his head; and the blow was terribly avenged, even by itself, for the jar caused the hammer to come down; the gun went off, sending the bullet downwards through the heart of the unfortunate man, who fell dead upon the ground. Eldredge[1] stood stupefied, looking at the catastrophe which had so suddenly occurred.

[1] Evidently a slip of the pen; Middleton being intended.

May 3d, Monday.—So here was the secret suddenly made safe in this so terrible way; its keepers reduced from two parties to one interest; the other who alone knew of this age-long mystery and trouble now carrying it into eternity, where a long line of those who partook of the knowledge, in each successive generation, might now be waiting to inquire of him how he had held his trust. He had kept it well, there was no doubt of it; for there he lay dead upon the ground, having betrayed it to no one, though by a method which none could have foreseen, the whole had come into the possession of him who had brought hither but half of it. Middleton looked down in horror upon the form that had just been so full of life and wrathful vigor—and now lay so quietly. Being wholly unconscious of any purpose to bring about the catastrophe, it had not at first struck him that his own position was in any manner affected by the violent death, under such circumstances, of the unfortunate man. But now it suddenly occurred to him, that there had been a train of incidents all calculated to make him the object of suspicion; and he felt that he could not, under the English administration of law, be suffered to go at large without rendering a strict account of himself and his relations with the deceased. He might, indeed, fly; he might still remain in the vicinity, and possibly escape notice. But was not the risk too great? Was it just even to be aware of this event, and not relate fully the manner of it, lest a suspicion of blood-guiltiness should rest upon some innocent head? But while he was thus cogitating, he heard footsteps approaching along the wood-path; and half-impulsively, half on purpose, he stept aside into the shrubbery, but still where he could see the dead body, and what passed near it.

The footsteps came on, and at the turning of the path, just where Middleton had met Eldredge, the new-comer appeared in sight. It was Hoper, in his usual dress of velveteen, looking now seedy, poverty-stricken, and altogether in ill-case, trudging moodily along, with his hat pulled over his brows, so that he did not see the ghastly object before him till his foot absolutely trod upon the dead man's hand. Being thus made aware of the proximity of the corpse, he started back a little, yet evincing such small emotion as did credit to his English reserve; then uttering a low exclamation,—cautiously low, indeed,—he stood looking at the corpse a moment or two, apparently in deep meditation. He then drew near, bent down, and without evincing any horror at the touch of death in this horrid shape, he opened the dead man's vest, inspected the wound, satisfied himself that life was extinct, and then nodded his head and smiled gravely. He next proceeded to examine seriatim the dead man's pockets, turning each of them inside out and taking the contents, where they appeared adapted to his needs: for instance, a silken purse, through the interstices of which some gold was visible; a watch, which however had been injured by the explosion, and had stopt just at the moment—twenty-one minutes past five—when the catastrophe took place. Hoper ascertained, by putting the watch to his ear, that this was the case; then pocketing it, he continued his researches. He likewise secured a note-book, on examining which he found several bank-notes, and some other papers. And having done this, the thief stood considering what to do next; nothing better occurring to him, he thrust the pockets back, gave the corpse as nearly as he could the same appearance that it had worn before he found it, and hastened away, leaving the horror there on the wood-path.

He had been gone only a few minutes when another step, a light woman's step, [was heard] coming along the pathway, and Alice appeared, having on her usual white mantle, straying along with that fearlessness which characterized her so strangely, and made her seem like one of the denizens of nature. She was singing in a low tone some one of those airs which have become so popular in England, as negro melodies; when suddenly, looking before her, she saw the blood-stained body on the grass, the face looking ghastly upward. Alice pressed her hand upon her heart; it was not her habit to scream, not the habit of that strong, wild, self-dependent nature; and the exclamation which broke from her was not for help, but the voice of her heart crying out to herself. For an instant she hesitated, as [if] not knowing what to do; then approached, and with her white, maiden hand felt the brow of the dead man, tremblingly, but yet firm, and satisfied herself that life had wholly departed. She pressed her hand, that had just touched the dead man's, on her forehead, and gave a moment to thought.

What her decision might have been, we cannot say, for while she stood in this attitude, Middleton stept from his seclusion, and at the noise of his approach she turned suddenly round, looking more frightened and agitated than at the moment when she had first seen the dead body. She faced Middleton, however, and looked him quietly in the eye. "You see this!" said she, gazing fixedly at him. "It is not at this moment that you first discover it."

"No," said Middleton, frankly. "It is not. I was present at the catastrophe. In one sense, indeed, I was the cause of it; but, Alice, I need not tell you that I am no murderer."

"A murderer?—no," said Alice, still looking at him with the same fixed gaze. "But you and this man were at deadly variance. He would have rejoiced at any chance that would have laid you cold and bloody on the earth, as he is now; nay, he would most eagerly have seized on any fair-looking pretext that would have given him a chance to stretch you there. The world will scarcely believe, when it knows all about your relations with him, that his blood is not on your hand. Indeed," said she, with a strange smile, "I see some of it there now!"

And, in very truth, so there was; a broad blood-stain that had dried on

Middleton's hand. He shuddered at it, but essayed vainly to rub it off.

"You see," said she. "It was foreordained that you should shed this man's blood; foreordained that, by digging into that old pit of pestilence, you should set the contagion loose again. You should have left it buried forever. But now what do you mean to do?"

"To proclaim this catastrophe," replied Middleton. "It is the only honest and manly way. What else can I do?"

"You can and ought to leave him on the wood-path, where he has fallen," said Alice, "and go yourself to take advantage of the state of things which Providence has brought about. Enter the old house, the hereditary house, where—now, at least—you alone have a right to tread. Now is the hour. All is within your grasp. Let the wrong of three hundred years be righted, and come back thus to your own, to these hereditary fields, this quiet, long-descended home; to title, to honor."

Yet as the wild maiden spoke thus, there was a sort of mockery in her eyes; on her brow; gleaming through all her face, as if she scorned what she thus pressed upon him, the spoils of the dead man who lay at their feet. Middleton, with his susceptibility, could not [but] be sensible of a wild and strange charm, as well as horror, in the situation; it seemed such a wonder that here, in formal, orderly, well-governed England, so wild a scene as this should have occurred; that they too [two?] should stand here, deciding on the descent of an estate, and the inheritance of a title, holding a court of their own.

"Come, then," said he, at length. "Let us leave this poor fallen antagonist in his blood, and go whither you will lead me. I will judge for myself. At all events, I will not leave my hereditary home without knowing what my power is."

"Come," responded Alice; and she turned back; but then returned and threw a handkerchief over the dead man's face, which while they spoke had assumed that quiet, ecstatic expression of joy which often is observed to overspread the faces of those who die of gunshot wounds, however fierce the passion in which the spirits took their flight. With this strange, grand, awful joy did the dead man gaze upward into the very eyes and hearts, as it were, of the two that now bent over him. They looked at one another.

"Whence comes this expression?" said Middleton, thoughtfully. "Alice, methinks he is reconciled to us now; and that we are members of one reconciled family, all of whom are in heaven but me."

Tuesday, May 4th.—"How strange is this whole situation between you and me," said Middleton, as they went up the winding pathway that led towards the house. "Shall I ever understand it? Do you mean ever to explain it to me? That I should find you here with that old man,[2] so mysterious, apparently so poor, yet so powerful! What [is] his relation to you?"

[2] The allusion here is apparently to the old man who proclaims himself Alice's father, in the portion dated April 14th. He figures hereafter as the old Hospitaller, Hammond. The reader must not take this present passage as referring to the death of Eldredge, which has just

taken place in the preceding section. The author is now beginning to elaborate the relation of Middleton and Alice. As will be seen, farther on, the death of Eldredge is ignored and abandoned; Eldredge is revived, and the story proceeds in another way.—G. P. L.

"A close one," replied Alice sadly. "He was my father!"

"Your father!" repeated Middleton, starting back. "It does but heighten the wonder! Your father! And yet, by all the tokens that birth and breeding, and habits of thought and native character can show, you are my countrywoman. That wild, free spirit was never born in the breast of an Englishwoman; that slight frame, that slender beauty, that frail envelopment of a quick, piercing, yet stubborn and patient spirit,—are those the properties of an English maiden?"

"Perhaps not," replied Alice quietly. "I am your countrywoman. My father was an American, and one of whom you have heard—and no good, alas!—for many a year."

"And who then was he?" asked Middleton.

"I know not whether you will hate me for telling you," replied Alice, looking him sadly though firmly in the face. "There was a man—long years since, in your childhood—whose plotting brain proved the ruin of himself and many another; a man whose great designs made him a sort of potentate, whose schemes became of national importance, and produced results even upon the history of the country in which he acted. That man was my father; a man who sought to do great things, and, like many who have had similar aims, disregarded many small rights, strode over them, on his way to effect a gigantic purpose. Among other men, your father was trampled under foot, ruined, done to death, even, by the effects of his ambition."

"How is it possible!" exclaimed Middleton. "Was it Wentworth?"

"Even so," said Alice, still with the same sad calmness and not withdrawing her steady eyes from his face. "After his ruin; after the catastrophe that overwhelmed him and hundreds more, he took to flight; guilty, perhaps, but guilty as a fallen conqueror is; guilty to such an extent that he ceased to be a cheat, as a conqueror ceases to be a murderer. He came to England. My father had an original nobility of nature; and his life had not been such as to debase it, but rather such as to cherish and heighten that self-esteem which at least keeps the possessor of it from many meaner vices. He took nothing with him; nothing beyond the bare means of flight, with the world before him, although thousands of gold would not have been missed out of the scattered fragments of ruin that lay around him. He found his way hither, led, as you were, by a desire to reconnect himself with the place whence his family had originated; for he, too, was of a race which had something to do with the ancient story which has now been brought to a close. Arrived here, there were circumstances that chanced to make his talents and habits of business available to this Mr. Eldredge, a man ignorant and indolent, unknowing how to make the best of the property that was in his hands. By degrees, he took the estate into his management, acquiring necessarily a preponderating influence over such a man."

"And you," said Middleton. "Have you been all along in England? For you must have been little more than an infant at the time."

"A mere infant," said Alice, "and I remained in our own country under the care of a relative who left me much to my own keeping; much to the influences of that wild culture which the freedom of our country gives to its youth. It is only two years that I have been in England."

"This, then," said Middleton thoughtfully, "accounts for much that has seemed so strange in the events through which we have passed; for the knowledge of my identity and my half-defined purpose which has always glided before me, and thrown so many strange shapes of difficulty in my path. But whence,—whence came that malevolence which your father's conduct has so unmistakably shown? I had done him no injury, though I had suffered much."

"I have often thought," replied Alice, "that my father, though retaining a preternatural strength and acuteness of intellect, was really not altogether sane. And, besides, he had made it his business to keep this estate, and all the complicated advantages of the representation of this old family, secure to the person who was deemed to have inherited them. A succession of ages and generations might be supposed to have blotted out your claims from existence; for it is not just that there should be no term of time which can make security for lack of fact and a few formalities. At all events, he had satisfied himself that his duty was to act as he has done."

"Be it so! I do not seek to throw blame on him," said Middleton.

"Besides, Alice, he was your father!"

"Yes," said she, sadly smiling; "let him [have] what protection that thought may give him, even though I lose what he may gain. And now here we are at the house. At last, come in! It is your own; there is none that can longer forbid you!"

They entered the door of the old mansion, now a farmhouse, and there were its old hall, its old chambers, all before them. They ascended the staircase, and stood on the landing-place above; while Middleton had again that feeling that had so often made him dizzy,—that sense of being in one dream and recognizing the scenery and events of a former dream. So overpowering was this feeling, that he laid his hand on the slender arm of Alice, to steady himself; and she comprehended the emotion that agitated him, and looked into his eyes with a tender sympathy, which she had never before permitted to be visible,—perhaps never before felt. He steadied himself and followed her till they had entered an ancient chamber, but one that was finished with all the comfortable luxury customary to be seen in English homes.

"Whither have you led me now?" inquired Middleton.

"Look round," said Alice. "Is there nothing here that you ought to recognize?—nothing that you kept the memory of, long ago?"

He looked round the room again and again, and at last, in a somewhat shadowy corner, he espied an old cabinet made of ebony and inlaid with pearl; one of those tall, stately, and elaborate pieces of furniture that are rather articles of architecture than upholstery; and on which a higher skill, feeling, and genius than now is ever employed on such things, was expended. Alice drew near the stately cabinet and threw wide the doors, which, like the portals of a palace, stood between two pillars; it all seemed to be unlocked, showing within some beautiful old pictures in the panel of the doors, and a mirror, that opened a long succession of mimic halls, reflection upon reflection, extending to an interminable nowhere.

"And what is this?" said Middleton,—"a cabinet? Why do you draw my attention so strongly to it?"

"Look at it well," said she. "Do you recognize nothing there? Have you forgotten your description? The stately palace with its architecture, each pillar with its architecture, those pilasters, that frieze; you ought to know them all. Somewhat less than you imagined in size, perhaps; a fairy reality, inches for yards; that is the only difference. And you have the key?"

And there then was that palace, to which tradition, so false at once and true, had given such magnitude and magnificence in the traditions of the Middleton family, around their shifting fireside in America. Looming afar through the mists of time, the little fact had become a gigantic vision. Yes, here it was in miniature, all that he had dreamed of; a palace of four feet high!

"You have the key of this palace," said Alice; "it has waited—that is, its secret and precious chamber has, for you to open it, these three hundred years. Do you know how to find that secret chamber?"

Middleton, still in that dreamy mood, threw open an inner door of the cabinet, and applying the old-fashioned key at his watch-chain to a hole in the mimic pavement within, pressed one of the mosaics, and immediately the whole floor of the apartment sank, and revealed a receptacle within. Alice had come forward eagerly, and they both looked into the hiding-place, expecting what should be there. It was empty! They looked into each other's faces with blank astonishment. Everything had been so strangely true, and so strangely false, up to this moment, that they could not comprehend this failure at the last moment. It was the strangest, saddest jest! It brought Middleton up with such a sudden revulsion that he grew dizzy, and the room swam round him and the cabinet dazzled before his eyes. It had been magnified to a palace; it had dwindled down to Liliputian size; and yet, up till now, it had seemed to contain in its diminutiveness all the riches which he had attributed to its magnitude. This last moment had utterly subverted it; the whole great structure seemed to vanish.

"See; here are the dust and ashes of it," observed Alice, taking something that was indeed only a pinch of dust out of the secret compartment. "There is nothing else."

II.

May 5th, Wednesday.—The father of these two sons, an aged man at the time, took much to heart their enmity; and after the catastrophe, he never held up his head again. He was not told that his son had perished, though such was the belief of the family; but imbibed the opinion that he had left his home and native land to become a wanderer on the face of the earth, and that some time or other he might return. In this idea he spent the remainder of his days; in this idea he died. It may be that the influence of this idea might be traced in the way in which he spent some of the latter years of his life, and a portion of the wealth which had become of little value in his eyes, since it had caused dissension and bloodshed between the sons of one household. It was a common mode of charity in those days—a common thing for rich men to do—to found an almshouse or a hospital, and endow it, for the support of a certain number of old and destitute men or women, generally such as had some claim of blood upon the founder, or at least were natives of the parish, the district, the county, where he dwelt. The Eldredge Hospital was founded for the benefit of twelve old men, who should have been wanderers upon the face of the earth; men, they should be, of some education, but defeated and hopeless, cast off by the world for misfortune, but not for crime. And this charity had subsisted, on terms varying little or nothing from the original ones, from that day to this; and, at this very time, twelve old men were not wanting, of various countries, of various fortunes, but all ending finally in ruin, who had centred here, to live on the poor pittance that had been assigned to them, three hundred years ago. What a series of chronicles it would have been if each of the beneficiaries of this charity, since its foundation, had left a record of the events which finally led him hither. Middleton often, as he talked with these old men, regretted that he himself had no turn for authorship, so rich a volume might he have compiled from the experience, sometimes sunny and triumphant, though always ending in shadow, which he gathered here. They were glad to talk to him, and would have been glad and grateful for any auditor, as they sat on one or another of the stone benches, in the sunshine of the garden; or at evening, around the great fireside, or within the chimney-corner, with their pipes and ale.

There was one old man who attracted much of his attention, by the venerableness of his aspect; by something dignified, almost haughty and commanding, in his air. Whatever might have been the intentions and expectations of the founder, it certainly had happened in these latter days that there was a difficulty in finding persons of education, of good manners, of evident respectability, to put into the places made vacant by deaths of members; whether that the paths of life are surer now than they used to be, and that men so arrange their lives as not to be left, in any event, quite without resources as they draw near its close; at any rate, there was a little tincture of the vagabond running through these twelve quasi gentlemen,—through several of them, at least. But this old man could not well be mistaken; in his manners, in his tones, in all his natural language and deportment, there was evidence that he had been more than respectable; and, viewing him, Middleton could not help wondering what statesman had suddenly vanished out of public life and taken refuge here, for his head was of the statesman-class, and his demeanor that of one who had exercised influence over large numbers of men. He sometimes endeavored to set on foot a familiar relation with this old man, but there was even a sternness in the manner in which he repelled these advances, that gave little encouragement for their renewal. Nor did it seem that his companions of the Hospital were more in his confidence than Middleton himself. They regarded him with a kind of awe, a shyness, and in most cases with a certain dislike, which denoted an imperfect understanding of him. To say the truth, there was not generally much love lost between any of the members of this family; they had met with too much disappointment in the world to take kindly, now, to one another or to anything or anybody. I rather suspect that they really had more pleasure in burying one another, when the time came, than in any other office of mutual kindness and brotherly love which it was their part to do; not out of hardness of heart, but merely from soured temper, and because, when people have met disappointment and have settled down into final unhappiness, with no more gush and spring of good spirits, there is nothing any more to create amiability out of.

So the old people were unamiable and cross to one another, and unamiable and cross to old Hammond, yet always with a certain respect; and the result seemed to be such as treated the old man well enough. And thus he moved about among them, a mystery; the histories of the others, in the general outline, were well enough known, and perhaps not very uncommon; this old man's history was known to none, except, of course, to the trustees of the charity, and to the Master of the Hospital, to whom it had necessarily been revealed, before the beneficiary could be admitted as an inmate. It was judged, by the deportment of the Master, that the old man had once held some eminent position in society; for, though bound to treat them all as gentlemen, he was thought to show an especial and solemn courtesy to Hammond.

Yet by the attraction which two strong and cultivated minds inevitably have for one another, there did spring up an acquaintanceship, an intercourse, between Middleton and this old man, which was followed up in many a conversation which they held together on all subjects that were supplied by the news of the day, or the history of the past. Middleton used to make the newspaper the opening for much discussion; and it seemed to him that the talk of his companion had much of the character of that of a retired statesman, on matters which, perhaps, he would look at all the more wisely, because it was impossible he could ever more have a personal agency in them. Their discussions sometimes turned upon the affairs of his own country, and its relations with the rest of the world, especially with England; and Middleton could not help being struck with the accuracy of the old man's knowledge respecting that country, which so few Englishmen know anything about; his shrewd appreciation of the American character,—shrewd and caustic, yet not without a good degree of justice; the sagacity of his remarks on the past, and prophecies of what was likely to happen,—prophecies which, in one instance, were singularly verified, in regard to a complexity which was then arresting the attention of both countries.

"You must have been in the United States," said he, one day.

"Certainly; my remarks imply personal knowledge," was the reply. "But it was before the days of steam."

"And not, I should imagine, for a brief visit," said Middleton. "I only wish the administration of this government had the benefit to-day of your knowledge of my countrymen. It might be better for both of these kindred nations."

"Not a whit," said the old man. "England will never understand America; for England never does understand a foreign country; and whatever you may say about kindred, America is as much a foreign country as France itself. These two hundred years of a different climate and circumstances— of life on a broad continent instead of in an island, to say nothing of the endless intermixture of nationalities in every part of the United States, except New England—have created a new and decidedly original type of national character. It is as well for both parties that they should not aim at any very intimate connection. It will never do."

"I should be sorry to think so," said Middleton; "they are at all events two noble breeds of men, and ought to appreciate one another. And America has the breadth of idea to do this for England, whether reciprocated or not."

Thursday, May 6th.—Thus Middleton was established in a singular way among these old men, in one of the surroundings most unlike anything in his own country. So old it was that it seemed to him the freshest and newest thing that he had ever met with. The residence was made infinitely the more interesting to him by the sense that he was near the place—as all the indications warned him—which he sought, whither his dreams had tended from his childhood; that he could wander each day round the park within which were the old gables of what he believed was his hereditary home. He had never known anything like the dreamy enjoyment of these days; so quiet, such a contrast to the turbulent life from which he had escaped across the sea. And here he set himself, still with that sense of shadowiness in what he saw and in what he did, in making all the researches possible to him, about the neighborhood; visiting every little church that raised its square battlemented Norman tower of gray stone, for several miles round about; making himself acquainted with each little village and hamlet that surrounded these churches, clustering about the graves of those who had dwelt in the same cottages aforetime. He visited all the towns within a dozen miles; and probably there were few of the inhabitants who had so good an acquaintance with the neighborhood as this native American attained within a few weeks after his coming thither.

In course of these excursions he had several times met with a young woman,—a young lady, one might term her, but in fact he was in some doubt what rank she might hold, in England,—who happened to be wandering about the country with a singular freedom. She was always alone, always on foot; he would see her sketching some picturesque old church, some ivied ruin, some fine drooping elm. She was a slight figure, much more so than English women generally are; and, though healthy of aspect, had not the ruddy complexion, which he was irreverently inclined to call the coarse tint, that is believed the great charm of English beauty. There was a freedom in her step and whole little womanhood, an elasticity, an irregularity, so to speak, that made her memorable from first sight; and when he had encountered her three or four times, he felt in a certain way acquainted with her. She was very simply dressed, and quite as simple in her deportment; there had been one or two occasions, when they had both smiled at the same thing; soon afterwards a little conversation had taken place between them; and thus, without any introduction, and in a way that somewhat puzzled Middleton himself, they had become acquainted. It was so unusual that a young English girl should be wandering about the country entirely alone—so much less usual that she should speak to a stranger—that Middleton scarcely knew how to account for it, but meanwhile accepted the fact readily and willingly, for in truth he found this mysterious personage a very likely and entertaining companion. There was a strange quality of boldness in her remarks, almost of brusqueness, that he might have expected to find in a young countrywoman of his own, if bred up among the strong-minded, but was astonished to find in a young Englishwoman. Somehow or other she made him think more of home than any other person or thing he met with; and he could not but feel that she was in strange contrast with everything about her. She was no beauty; very piquant; very pleasing; in some points of view and at some moments pretty; always good-humored, but somewhat too self-possessed for Middleton's taste. It struck him that she had talked with him as if she had some knowledge of him and of the purposes with which he was there; not that this was expressed, but only implied by the fact that, on looking back to what had passed, he found many strange coincidences in what she had said with what he was thinking about.

He perplexed himself much with thinking whence this young woman had come, where she belonged, and what might be her history; when, the next day, he again saw her, not this time rambling on foot, but seated in an open barouche with a young lady. Middleton lifted his hat to her, and she nodded and smiled to him; and it appeared to Middleton that a conversation ensued about him with the young lady, her companion. Now, what still more interested him was the fact that, on the panel of the barouche were the arms of the family now in possession of the estate of Smithell's; so that the young lady, his new acquaintance, or the young lady, her seeming friend, one or the other, was the sister of the present owner of that estate. He was inclined to think that his acquaintance could not be the Miss Eldredge, of whose beauty he had heard many tales among the people of the neighborhood. The other young lady, a tall, reserved, fair-haired maiden, answered the description considerably better. He concluded, therefore, that his acquaintance must be a visitor, perhaps a dependent and companion; though the freedom of her thought, action, and way of life seemed hardly consistent with this idea. However, this slight incident served to give him a sort of connection with the family, and he could but hope that some further chance would introduce him within what he fondly called his hereditary walls. He had come to think of this as a dreamland; and it seemed even more a dreamland now than before it rendered itself into actual substance, an old house of stone and timber standing within its park, shaded about with its ancestral trees.

But thus, at all events, he was getting himself a little wrought into the net-work of human life around him, secluded as his position had at first seemed to be, in the farmhouse where he had taken up his lodgings. For, there was the Hospital and its old inhabitants, in whose monotonous existence he soon came to pass for something, with his liveliness of mind, his experience, his good sense, his patience as a listener, his comparative youth even—his power of adapting himself to these stiff and crusty characters, a power learned among other things in his political life, where he had acquired something of the faculty (good or bad as might be) of making himself all things to all men. But though he amused himself with them all, there was in truth but one man among them in whom he really felt much interest; and that one, we need hardly say, was Hammond. It was not often that he found the old gentleman in a conversible mood; always courteous, indeed, but generally cool and reserved; often engaged in his one room, to which Middleton had never yet been admitted, though he had more than once sent in his name, when Hammond was not apparent upon the bench which, by common consent of the Hospital, was appropriated to him.

One day, however, notwithstanding that the old gentleman was confined to his room by indisposition, he ventured to inquire at the door, and, considerably to his surprise, was admitted. He found Hammond in his easy-chair, at a table, with writing-materials before him; and as Middleton entered, the old gentleman looked at him with a stern, fixed regard, which, however, did not seem to imply any particular displeasure towards this visitor, but rather a severe way of regarding mankind in general. Middleton looked curiously around the small apartment, to see what modification the character of the man had had upon the customary furniture of the Hospital, and how much of individuality he had given to that general type. There was a shelf of books, and a row of them on the mantel-piece; works of political economy, they appeared to be, statistics and things of that sort; very dry reading, with which, however, Middleton's experience as a politician had made him acquainted. Besides these there were a few works on local antiquities, a county-history borrowed from the Master's library, in which Hammond appeared to have been lately reading.

"They are delightful reading," observed Middleton, "these old county-histories, with their great folio volumes and their minute account of the affairs of families and the genealogies, and descents of estates, bestowing as much blessed space on a few hundred acres as other historians give to a principality. I fear that in my own country we shall never have anything of this kind. Our space is so vast that we shall never come to know and love it, inch by inch, as the English antiquarians do the tracts of country with which they deal; and besides, our land is always likely to lack the interest that belongs to English

42

estates; for where land changes its ownership every few years, it does not become imbued with the personalities of the people who live on it. It is but so much grass; so much dirt, where a succession of people have dwelt too little to make it really their own. But I have found a pleasure that I had no conception of before, in reading some of the English local histories."

"It is not a usual course of reading for a transitory visitor," said

Hammond. "What could induce you to undertake it?"

"Simply the wish, so common and natural with Americans," said Middleton—"the wish to find out something about my kindred—the local origin of my own family."

"You do not show your wisdom in this," said his visitor. "America had better recognize the fact that it has nothing to do with England, and look upon itself as other nations and people do, as existing on its own hook. I never heard of any people looking hack to the country of their remote origin in the way the Anglo-Americans do. For instance, England is made up of many alien races, German, Danish. Norman, and what not: it has received large accessions of population at a later date than the settlement of the United States. Yet these families melt into the great homogeneous mass of Englishmen, and look hack no more to any other country. There are in this vicinity many descendants of the French Huguenots; but they care no more for France than for Timbuctoo, reckoning themselves only Englishmen, as if they were descendants of the aboriginal Britons. Let it be so with you."

"So it might be," replied Middleton, "only that our relations with England remain far more numerous than our disconnections, through the bonds of history, of literature, of all that makes up the memories, and much that makes up the present interests of a people. And therefore I must still continue to pore over these old folios, and hunt around these precincts, spending thus the little idle time I am likely to have in a busy life. Possibly finding little to my purpose; but that is quite a secondary consideration."

"If you choose to tell me precisely what your aims are," said Hammond, "it is possible I might give you some little assistance."

May 7th, Friday.—Middleton was in fact more than half ashamed of the dreams which he had cherished before coming to England, and which since, at times, had been very potent with him, assuming as strong a tinge of reality as those [scenes?] into which he had strayed. He could not prevail with himself to disclose fully to this severe, and, as he thought, cynical old man how strong within him was the sentiment that impelled him to connect himself with the old life of England, to join on the broken thread of ancestry and descent, and feel every link well established. But it seemed to him that he ought not to lose this fair opportunity of gaining some light on the abstruse field of his researches; and he therefore explained to Hammond that he had reason, from old family traditions, to believe that he brought with him a fragment of a history that, if followed out, might lead to curious results. He told him, in a tone half serious, what he had heard respecting the quarrel of the two brothers, and the Bloody Footstep, the impress of which was said to remain, as a lasting memorial of the tragic termination of that enmity. At this point, Hammond interrupted him. He had indeed, at various points of the narrative, nodded and smiled mysteriously, as if looking into his mind and seeing something there analogous to what he was listening to. He now spoke.

"This is curious," said he. "Did you know that there is a manor-house in this neighborhood, the family of which prides itself on having such a blood-stained threshold as you have now described?"

"No, indeed!" exclaimed Middleton, greatly interested. "Where?"

"It is the old manor-house of Smithell's," replied Hammond, "one of those old wood and timber [plaster?] mansions, which are among the most ancient specimens of domestic architecture in England. The house has now passed into the female line, and by marriage has been for two or three generations in possession of another family. But the blood of the old inheritors is still in the family. The house itself, or portions of it, are thought to date back quite as far as the Conquest."

"Smithell's?" said Middleton. "Why, I have seen that old house from a distance, and have felt no little interest in its antique aspect. And it has a Bloody Footstep! Would it be possible for a stranger to get an opportunity to inspect it?"

"Unquestionably," said Hammond; "nothing easier. It is but a moderate distance from here, and if you can moderate your young footsteps, and your American quick walk, to an old man's pace, I would go there with you some day. In this languor and ennui of my life, I spend some time in local antiquarianism, and perhaps I might assist you in tracing out how far these traditions of yours may have any connection with reality. It would be curious, would it not, if you had come, after two hundred years, to piece out a story which may have been as much a mystery in England as there in America?"

An engagement was made for a walk to Smithell's the ensuing day; and meanwhile Middleton entered more fully into what he had received from family traditions and what he had thought out for himself on the matter in question.

"Are you aware," asked Hammond, "that there was formerly a title in this family, now in abeyance, and which the heirs have at various times claimed, and are at this moment claiming? Do you know, too,—but you can scarcely know it,—that it has been surmised by some that there is an insecurity in the title to the estate, and has always been; so that the possessors have lived in some apprehension, from time immemorial, that another heir would appear and take from them the fair inheritance? It is a singular coincidence."

"Very strange," exclaimed Middleton. "No; I was not aware of it; and, to say the truth, I should not altogether like to come forward in the light of a claimant. But this is a dream, surely!"

"I assure you, sir," continued the old man, "that you come here in a very critical moment; and singularly enough there is a perplexity, a difficulty, that has endured for as long a time as when your ancestors emigrated, that is still rampant within the bowels, as I may say, of the family. Of course, it is too like a romance that you should be able to establish any such claim as would have a valid influence on this matter; but still, being here on the spot, it may be worth while, if merely as a matter of amusement, to make some researches into this matter."

"Surely I will," said Middleton, with a smile, which concealed more earnestness than he liked to show; "as to the title, a Republican cannot be supposed to think twice about such a bagatelle. The estate!—that might be a more serious consideration."

They continued to talk on the subject; and Middleton learned that the present possessor of the estates was a gentleman nowise distinguished from hundreds of other English gentlemen; a country squire modified in accordance with the type of to-day, a frank, free, friendly sort of a person enough, who had travelled on the Continent, who employed himself much in field-sports, who was unmarried, and had a sister who was reckoned among the beauties of the county.

While the conversation was thus going on, to Middleton's astonishment there came a knock at the door of the room, and, without waiting for a response, it was opened, and there appeared at it the same young woman whom he had already met. She came in with perfect freedom and familiarity, and was received quietly by the old gentleman; who, however, by his manner towards Middleton, indicated that he was now to take his leave. He did so, after settling the hour at which the excursion of the next day was to take place. This arranged, he departed, with much to think of, and a light glimmering through the confused labyrinth of thoughts which had been unilluminated hitherto.

To say the truth, he questioned within himself whether it were not better to get as quickly as he could out of the vicinity; and, at any rate, not to put anything of earnest in what had hitherto been nothing more than a romance to him. There was something very dark and sinister in the events of family history, which now assumed a reality that they had never before worn; so much tragedy, so much hatred, had been thrown into that deep pit, and buried under the accumulated debris, the fallen leaves, the rust and dust of more than two centuries, that it seemed not worth while to dig it up; for perhaps the deadly influences, which it had taken so much time to hide, might still be lurking there, and become potent if he now uncovered them. There was something that startled him, in the strange, wild light, which gleamed from the old man's eyes, as he threw out the suggestions which had opened this prospect to him. What right had he—an American, Republican, disconnected with this country so long, alien from its habits of thought and life, reverencing none of the things which Englishmen reverenced—what right had he to come with these musty claims from the dim past, to disturb them in the life that belonged to them? There was a higher and a deeper law than any connected with ancestral claims which he could assert; and he had an idea that the law bade him keep to the country which his ancestor had chosen and to its institutions, and not meddle nor make with England. The roots of his family tree could not reach under the ocean; he was at most but a seedling from the parent tree. While thus meditating he found that his footsteps had brought him unawares within sight of the old manor-house of Smithell's; and that he was wandering in a path which, if he followed it further, would bring him to an entrance in one of the wings of the mansion. With a sort of shame upon him, he went forward, and, leaning against a tree, looked at what he considered the home of his ancestors.

May 9th, Sunday.—At the time appointed, the two companions set out on their little expedition, the old man in his Hospital uniform, the long black mantle, with the bear and ragged staff engraved in silver on the breast, and Middleton in the plain costume which he had adopted in these wanderings about the country. On their way, Hammond was not very communicative, occasionally dropping some shrewd remark with a good deal of acidity in it; now and then, too, favoring his companion with some reminiscence of local antiquity; but oftenest silent. Thus they went on, and entered the park of Pemberton Manor by a by-path, over a stile and one of those footways, which are always so well worth threading out in England, leading the pedestrian into picturesque and characteristic scenes, when the highroad would show him nothing except what was commonplace and uninteresting. Now the gables of the old manor-house appeared before them, rising amidst the hereditary woods, which doubtless dated from a time beyond the days which Middleton fondly recalled, when his ancestors had walked beneath their shade. On each side of them were thickets and copses of fern, amidst which they saw the hares peeping out to gaze upon them, occasionally running across the path, and comporting themselves like creatures that felt themselves under some sort of protection from the outrages of man, though they knew too much of his destructive character to trust him too far. Pheasants, too, rose close beside them, and winged but a little way before they alighted; they likewise knew, or seemed to know, that their hour was not yet come. On all sides in these woods, these wastes, these beasts and birds, there was a character that was neither wild nor tame. Man had laid his grasp on them all, and done enough to redeem them from barbarism, but had stopped short of domesticating them; although Nature, in the wildest thing there, acknowledged the powerful and pervading influence of cultivation.

Arriving at a side door of the mansion, Hammond rang the bell, and a servant soon appeared. He seemed to know the old man, and immediately acceded to his request to be permitted to show his companion the house; although it was not precisely a show-house, nor was this the hour when strangers were usually admitted. They entered; and the servant did not give himself the trouble to act as a cicerone to the two visitants, but carelessly said to the old gentleman that he knew the rooms, and that he would leave him to discourse to his friend about them. Accordingly, they went into the old hall, a dark oaken-panelled room, of no great height, with many doors opening into it. There was a fire burning on the hearth; indeed, it was the custom of the house to keep it up from morning to night; and in the damp, chill climate of England, there is seldom a day in some part of which a fire is not pleasant to feel. Hammond here pointed out a stuffed fox, to which some story of a famous chase was attached; a pair of antlers of enormous size; and some old family pictures, so blackened with time and neglect that Middleton could not well distinguish their features, though curious to do so, as hoping to see there the lineaments of some with whom he might claim kindred. It was a venerable apartment, and gave a good foretaste of what they might hope to find in the rest of the mansion.

But when they had inspected it pretty thoroughly, and were ready to proceed, an elderly gentleman entered the hall, and, seeing Hammond, addressed him in a kindly, familiar way; not indeed as an equal friend, but with a pleasant and not irksome conversation. "I am glad to see you here again," said he. "What? I have an hour of leisure; for, to say the truth, the day hangs rather heavy till the shooting season begins. Come; as you have a friend with you, I will be your cicerone myself about the house, and show you whatever mouldy objects of interest it contains."

48

He then graciously noticed the old man's companion, but without asking or seeming to expect an introduction; for, after a careless glance at him, he had evidently set him down as a person without social claims, a young man in the rank of life fitted to associate with an inmate of Pemberton's Hospital. And it must be noticed that his treatment of Middleton was not on that account the less kind, though far from being so elaborately courteous as if he had met him as an equal. "You have had something of a walk," said he, "and it is a rather hot day. The beer of Pemberton Manor has been reckoned good these hundred years; will you taste it?"

Hammond accepted the offer, and the beer was brought in a foaming tankard; but Middleton declined it, for in truth there was a singular emotion in his breast, as if the old enmity, the ancient injuries, were not yet atoned for, and as if he must not accept the hospitality of one who represented his hereditary foe. He felt, too, as if there were something unworthy, a certain want of fairness, in entering clandestinely the house, and talking with its occupant under a veil, as it were; and had he seen clearly how to do it, he would perhaps at that moment have fairly told Mr. Eldredge that he brought with him the character of kinsman, and must be received on that grade or none. But it was not easy to do this; and after all, there was no clear reason why he should do it; so he let the matter pass, merely declining to take the refreshment, and keeping himself quiet and retired.

Squire Eldredge seemed to be a good, ordinary sort of gentleman, reasonably well educated, and with few ideas beyond his estate and neighborhood, though he had once held a seat in Parliament for part of a term. Middleton could not but contrast him, with an inward smile, with the shrewd, alert politicians, their faculties all sharpened to the utmost, whom he had known and consorted with in the American Congress. Hammond had slightly informed him that his companion was an American; and Mr. Eldredge immediately gave proof of the extent of his knowledge of that country, by inquiring whether he came from the State of New England, and whether Mr. Webster was still President of the United States; questions to which Middleton returned answers that led to no further conversation. These little preliminaries over, they continued their ramble through the house, going through tortuous passages, up and down little flights of steps, and entering chambers that had all the charm of discoveries of hidden regions; loitering about, in short, in a labyrinth calculated to put the head into a delightful confusion. Some of these rooms contained their time-honored furniture, all in the best possible repair, heavy, dark, polished; beds that had been marriage beds and dying beds over and over again; chairs with carved backs; and all manner of old world curiosities; family pictures, and samplers, and embroidery; fragments of tapestry; an inlaid floor; everything having a story to it, though, to say the truth, the possessor of these curiosities made but a bungling piece of work in telling the legends connected with them. In one or two instances Hammond corrected him.

By and by they came to what had once been the principal bed-room of the house; though its gloom, and some circumstances of family misfortune that had happened long ago, had caused it to fall into disrepute in latter times; and it was now called the Haunted Chamber, or the Ghost's Chamber. The furniture of this room, however, was particularly rich in its antique magnificence; and one of the principal objects was a great black cabinet of ebony and ivory, such as may often be seen in old English houses, and perhaps often in the palaces of Italy, in which country they perhaps originated. This present cabinet was known to have been in the house as long ago as the reign of Queen Elizabeth, and how much longer neither tradition nor record told. Hammond particularly directed Middleton's attention to it.

"There is nothing in this house," said he, "better worth your attention than that cabinet.' Consider its plan; it represents a stately mansion, with pillars, an entrance, with a lofty flight of steps, windows, and everything perfect. Examine it well."

There was such an emphasis in the old man's way of speaking that Middleton turned suddenly round from all that he had been looking at, and fixed his whole attention on the cabinet; and strangely enough, it seemed to be the representative, in small, of something that he had seen in a dream. To say the truth, if some cunning workman had been employed to copy his idea of the old family mansion, on a scale of half an inch to a yard, and in ebony and ivory instead of stone, he could not have produced a closer imitation. Everything was there.

"This is miraculous!" exclaimed he. "I do not understand it."

"Your friend seems to be curious in these matters," said Mr. Eldredge graciously. "Perhaps he is of some trade that makes this sort of manufacture particularly interesting to him. You are quite at liberty, my friend, to open the cabinet and inspect it as minutely as you wish. It is an article that has a good deal to do with an obscure portion of our family history. Look, here is the key, and the mode of opening the outer door of the palace, as we may well call it." So saying, he threw open the outer door, and disclosed within the mimic likeness of a stately entrance hall, with a floor chequered of ebony and ivory. There were other doors that seemed to open into apartments in the interior of the palace; but when Mr. Eldredge threw them likewise wide, they proved to be drawers and secret receptacles, where papers, jewels, money, anything that it was desirable to store away secretly, might be kept.

"You said, sir," said Middleton, thoughtfully, "that your family history contained matter of interest in reference to this cabinet. Might I inquire what those legends are?"

"Why, yes," said Mr. Eldredge, musing a little. "I see no reason why I should have any idle concealment about the matter, especially to a foreigner and a man whom I am never likely to see again. You must know, then, my friend, that there was once a time when this cabinet was known to contain the fate of the estate and its possessors; and if it had held all that it was supposed to hold, I should not now be the lord of Pemberton Manor, nor the claimant of an ancient title. But my father, and his father before him, and his father besides, have held the estate and prospered on it; and I think we may fairly conclude now that the cabinet contains nothing except what we see."

And he rapidly again threw open one after another all the numerous drawers and receptacles of the cabinet.

"It is an interesting object," said Middleton, after looking very closely and with great attention at it, being pressed thereto, indeed, by the owner's good natured satisfaction in possessing this rare article of vertu. "It is admirable work," repeated he, drawing back. "That mosaic floor, especially, is done with an art and skill that I never saw equalled."

There was something strange and altered in Middleton's tones, that attracted the notice of Mr. Eldredge. Looking at him, he saw that he had grown pale, and had a rather bewildered air.

"Is your friend ill?" said he. "He has not our English ruggedness of look. He would have done better to take a sip of the cool tankard, and a slice of the cold beef. He finds no such food and drink as that in his own country, I warrant."

"His color has come back," responded Hammond, briefly. "He does not need any refreshment, I think, except, perhaps, the open air."

In fact, Middleton, recovering himself, apologized to Mr. Hammond [Eldredge?]; and as they had now seen nearly the whole of the house, the two visitants took their leave, with many kindly offers on Mr. Eldredge's part to permit the young man to view the cabinet whenever he wished. As they went out of the house (it was by another door than that which gave them entrance), Hammond laid his hand on Middleton's shoulder and pointed to a stone on the threshold, on which he was about to set his foot. "Take care!" said he. "It is the Bloody Footstep."

Middleton looked down and saw something, indeed, very like the shape of a footprint, with a hue very like that of blood. It was a twilight sort of a place, beneath a porch, which was much overshadowed by trees and shrubbery. It might have been blood; but he rather thought, in his wicked skepticism, that it was a natural, reddish stain in the stone. He measured his own foot, however, in the Bloody Footstep, and went on.

May 10th, Monday.—This is the present aspect of the story: Middleton is the descendant of a family long settled in the United States; his ancestor having emigrated to New England with the Pilgrims; or, perhaps, at a still earlier date, to Virginia with Raleigh's colonists. There had been a family dissension,—a bitter hostility between two brothers in England; on account, probably, of a love affair, the two both being attached to the same lady. By the influence of the family on both sides, the young lady had formed an engagement with the elder brother, although her affections had settled on the younger. The marriage was about to take place when the younger brother and the bride both disappeared, and were never heard of with any certainty afterwards; but it was believed at the time that he had been killed, and in proof of it a bloody footstep remained on the threshold of the ancestral mansion. There were rumors, afterwards, traditionally continued to the present day, that the younger brother and the bride were seen, and together, in England; and that some voyager across the sea had found them living together, husband and wife, on the other side of the Atlantic. But the elder brother became a moody and reserved man, never married, and left the inheritance to the children of a third brother, who then became the representative of the family in England; and the better authenticated story was that the second brother had really been slain, and that the young lady (for all the parties may have been Catholic) had gone to the Continent and taken the veil there. Such was the family history as known or surmised in England, and in the neighborhood of the manor-house, where the Bloody Footstep still remained on the threshold; and the posterity of the third brother still held the estate, and perhaps were claimants of an ancient baronage, long in abeyance.

Now, on the other side of the Atlantic, the second brother and the young lady had really been married, and became the parents of a posterity, still extant, of which the Middleton of the romance is the surviving male. Perhaps he had changed his name, being so much tortured with the evil and wrong that had sprung up in his family, so remorseful, so outraged, that he wished to disconnect himself with all the past, and begin life quite anew in a new world. But both he and his wife, though happy in one another, had been remorsefully and sadly so; and, with such feelings, they had never again communicated with their respective families, nor had given their children the means of doing so. There must, I think, have been something nearly approaching to guilt on the second brother's part, and the bride should have broken a solemnly plighted troth to the elder brother, breaking away from him when almost his wife. The elder brother had been known to have been wounded at the time of the second brother's disappearance; and it had been the surmise that he had received this hurt in the personal conflict in which the latter was slain. But in truth the second brother had stabbed him in the emergency of being discovered in the act of escaping with the bride; and this was what weighed upon his conscience throughout life in America. The

American family had prolonged itself through various fortunes, and all the ups and downs incident to our institutions, until the present day. They had some old family documents, which had been rather carelessly kept; but the present representative, being an educated man, had looked over them, and found one which interested him strongly. It was—what was it?—perhaps a copy of a letter written by his ancestor on his death-bed, telling his real name, and relating the above incidents. These incidents had come down in a vague, wild way, traditionally, in the American family, forming a wondrous and incredible legend, which Middleton had often laughed at, yet been greatly interested in; and the discovery of this document seemed to give a certain aspect of veracity and reality to the tradition. Perhaps, however, the document only related to the change of name, and made reference to certain evidences by which, if any descendant of the family should deem it expedient, he might prove his hereditary identity. The legend must be accounted for by having been gathered from the talk of the first ancestor and his wife. There must be in existence, in the early records of the colony, an authenticated statement of this change of name, and satisfactory proofs that the American family, long known as Middleton, were really a branch of the English family of Eldredge, or whatever. And in the legend, though not in the written document, there must be an account of a certain magnificent, almost palatial residence, which Middleton shall presume to be the ancestral home; and in this palace there shall be said to be a certain secret chamber, or receptacle, where is reposited a document that shall complete the evidence of the genealogical descent.

Middleton is still a young man, but already a distinguished one in his own country; he has entered early into politics, been sent to Congress, but having met with some disappointments in his ambitious hopes, and being disgusted with the fierceness of political contests in our country, he has come abroad for recreation and rest. His imagination has dwelt much, in his boyhood, on the legendary story of his family; and the discovery of the document has revived these dreams. He determines to search out the family mansion; and thus he arrives, bringing half of a story, being the only part known in America, to join it on to the other half, which is the only part known in England. In an introduction I must do the best I can to state his side of the matter to the reader, he having communicated it to me in a friendly way, at the Consulate; as many people have communicated quite as wild pretensions to English genealogies.

He comes to the midland counties of England, where he conceives his claims to lie, and seeks for his ancestral home; but there are difficulties in the way of finding it, the estates having passed into the female line, though still remaining in the blood. By and by, however, he comes to an old town where there is one of the charitable institutions bearing the name of his family, by whose beneficence it had indeed been founded, in Queen Elizabeth's time. He of course becomes interested in this Hospital; he finds it still going on, precisely as it did in the old days; and all the character and life of the establishment must be picturesquely described. Here he gets acquainted with an old man, an inmate of the Hospital, who (if the uncontrollable fatality of the story will permit) must have an active influence on the ensuing events. I suppose him to have been an American, but to have fled his country and taken refuge in England; he shall have been a man of the Nicholas Biddle stamp, a mighty speculator, the ruin of whose schemes had crushed hundreds of people, and Middleton's father among the rest. Here he had quitted the activity of his mind, as well as he could, becoming a local antiquary, etc., and he has made himself acquainted with the family history of the Eldredges, knowing more about it than the members of the family themselves do. He had known in America (from Middleton's father, who was his friend) the legends preserved in this branch of the family, and perhaps had been struck by the way in which they fit into the English legends; at any rate, this strikes him when Middleton tells him his story and shows him the document respecting the change of name. After various conversations together (in which, however, the old man keeps the secret of his own identity, and indeed acts as mysteriously as possible), they go together to visit the ancestral mansion. Perhaps it should not be in their first visit that the cabinet, representing the stately mansion, shall be seen. But the Bloody Footstep may; which shall interest Middleton much, both because Hammond has told him the English tradition respecting it, and because too the legends of the American family made some obscure allusions to his ancestor having left blood—a bloody footstep—on the ancestral threshold. This is the point to which the story has now been sketched out. Middleton finds a commonplace old English country

55

gentleman in possession of the estate, where his forefathers have lived in peace for many generations; but there must be circumstances contrived which shall cause Middleton's conduct to be attended by no end of turmoil and trouble. The old Hospitaller, I suppose, must be the malicious agent in this; and his malice must be motived in some satisfactory way. The more serious question, what shall be the nature of this tragic trouble, and how can it be brought about?

May 11th, Tuesday.—How much better would it have been if this secret, which seemed so golden, had remained in the obscurity in which two hundred years had buried it! That deep, old, grass-grown grave being opened, out from it streamed into the sunshine the old fatalities, the old crimes, the old misfortunes, the sorrows, that seemed to have departed from the family forever. But it was too late now to close it up; he must follow out the thread that led him on,—the thread of fate, if you choose to call it so; but rather the impulse of an evil will, a stubborn self-interest, a desire for certain objects of ambition which were preferred to what yet were recognized as real goods. Thus reasoned, thus raved, Eldredge, as he considered the things that he had done, and still intended to do; nor did these perceptions make the slightest difference in his plans, nor in the activity with which he set about their performance. For this purpose he sent for his lawyer, and consulted him on the feasibility of the design which he had already communicated to him respecting Middleton. But the man of law shook his head, and, though deferentially, declined to have any active concern with the matter that threatened to lead him beyond the bounds which he allowed himself, into a seductive but perilous region.

"My dear sir," said he, with some earnestness, "you had much better content yourself with such assistance as I can professionally and consistently give you. Believe [me], I am willing to do a lawyer's utmost, and to do more would be as unsafe for the client as for the legal adviser."

Thus left without an agent and an instrument, this unfortunate man had to meditate on what means he would use to gain his ends through his own unassisted efforts. In the struggle with himself through which he had passed, he had exhausted pretty much all the feelings that he had to bestow

56

on this matter; and now he was ready to take hold of almost any temptation that might present itself, so long as it showed a good prospect of success and a plausible chance of impunity. While he was thus musing, he heard a female voice chanting some song, like a bird's among the pleasant foliage of the trees, and soon he saw at the end of a wood-walk Alice, with her basket on her arm, passing on toward the village. She looked towards him as she passed, but made no pause nor yet hastened her steps, not seeming to think it worth her while to be influenced by him. He hurried forward and overtook her.

So there was this poor old gentleman, his comfort utterly overthrown, decking his white hair and wrinkled brow with the semblance of a coronet, and only hoping that the reality might crown and bless him before he was laid in the ancestral tomb. It was a real calamity; though by no means the greatest that had been fished up out of the pit of domestic discord that had been opened anew by the advent of the American; and by the use which had been made of it by the cantankerous old man of the Hospital. Middleton, as he looked at these evil consequences, sometimes regretted that he had not listened to those forebodings which had warned him back on the eve of his enterprise; yet such was the strange entanglement and interest which had wound about him, that often he rejoiced that for once he was engaged in something that absorbed him fully, and the zeal for the development of which made him careless for the result in respect to its good or evil, but only desirous that it show itself. As for Alice, she seemed to skim lightly through all these matters, whether as a spirit of good or ill he could not satisfactorily judge. He could not think her wicked; yet her actions seemed unaccountable on the plea that she was otherwise. It was another characteristic thread in the wild web of madness that had spun itself about all the prominent characters of our story. And when Middleton thought of these things, he felt as if it might be his duty (supposing he had the power) to shovel the earth again into the pit that he had been the means of opening; but also felt that, whether duty or not, he would never perform it.

For, you see, on the American's arrival he had found the estate in the hands of one of the descendants; but some disclosures consequent on his arrival had thrown it into the hands of another; or, at all events, had seemed to make it apparent that justice required that it should be so disposed of. No sooner was the discovery made than the possessor put on a coronet; the new heir had commenced legal proceedings; the sons of the respective branches had come to blows and blood; and the devil knows what other devilish consequences had ensued. Besides this, there was much falling in love at cross-purposes, and a general animosity of everybody against everybody else, in proportion to the closeness of the natural ties and their obligation to love one another.

The moral, if any moral were to be gathered from these petty and wretched circumstances, was, "Let the past alone: do not seek to renew it; press on to higher and better things,—at all events, to other things; and be assured that the right way can never be that which leads you back to the identical shapes that you long ago left behind. Onward, onward, onward!"

"What have you to do here?" said Alice. "Your lot is in another land. You have seen the birthplace of your forefathers, and have gratified your natural yearning for it; now return, and cast in your lot with your own people, let it be what it will. I fully believe that it is such a lot as the world has never yet seen, and that the faults, the weaknesses, the errors, of your countrymen will vanish away like morning mists before the rising sun. You can do nothing better than to go back."

"This is strange advice, Alice," said Middleton, gazing at her and smiling. "Go back, with such a fair prospect before me; that were strange indeed! It is enough to keep me here, that here only I shall see you,—enough to make me rejoice to have come, that I have found you here."

"Do not speak in this foolish way," cried Alice, panting. "I am giving you the best advice, and speaking in the wisest way I am capable of,—speaking on good grounds too,—and you turn me aside with a silly compliment. I tell you that this is no comedy in which we are performers, but a deep, sad tragedy; and that it depends most upon you whether or no it shall be pressed to a catastrophe. Think well of it."

"I have thought, Alice," responded the young man, "and I must let things take their course; if, indeed, it depends at all upon me, which I see no present reason to suppose. Yet I wish you would explain to me what you mean."

To take up the story from the point where we left it: by the aid of the American's revelations, some light is thrown upon points of family history, which induce the English possessor of the estate to suppose that the time has come for asserting his claim to a title which has long been in abeyance. He therefore sets about it, and engages in great expenses, besides contracting the enmity of many persons, with whose interests he interferes. A further complication is brought about by the secret interference of the old Hospitaller, and Alice goes singing and dancing through the whole, in a way that makes her seem like a beautiful devil, though finally it will be recognized that she is an angel of light. Middleton, half bewildered, can scarcely tell how much of this is due to his own agency; how much is independent of him and would have happened had he stayed on his own side of the water. By and by a further and unexpected development presents the singular fact that he himself is the heir to whatever claims there are, whether of property or rank,—all centring in him as the representative of the eldest brother. On this discovery there ensues a tragedy in the death of the present possessor of the estate, who has staked everything upon the issue; and Middleton, standing amid the ruin and desolation of which he has been the innocent cause, resigns all the claims which he might now assert, and retires, arm in arm with Alice, who has encouraged him to take this course, and to act up to his character. The estate takes a passage into the female line, and the old name becomes extinct, nor does Middleton seek to continue it by resuming it in place of the one long ago assumed by his ancestor. Thus he and his wife become the Adam and Eve of a new epoch, and the fitting missionaries of a new social faith, of which there must be continual hints through the book.

A knot of characters may be introduced as gathering around Middleton, comprising expatriated Americans of all sorts: the wandering printer who came to me so often at the Consulate, who said he was a native of Philadelphia, and could not go home in the thirty years that he had been trying to do so, for lack of the money to pay his passage; the large banker; the consul of Leeds; the woman asserting her claims to half Liverpool; the gifted literary lady, maddened by Shakespeare, &c., &c. The Yankee who had been driven insane by the Queen's notice, slight as it was, of the photographs of his two children which he had sent her. I have not yet struck the true keynote of this Romance, and until I do, and unless I do, I shall write nothing but tediousness and nonsense. I do not wish it to be a picture of life, but a Romance, grim, grotesque, quaint, of which the Hospital might be the fitting scene. It might have so much of the hues of life that the reader should sometimes think it was intended for a picture, yet the atmosphere should be such as to excuse all wildness. In the Introduction, I might disclaim all intention to draw a real picture, but say that the continual meetings I had with Americans bent on such errands had suggested this wild story. The descriptions of scenery, &c., and of the Hospital, might be correct, but there should be a tinge of the grotesque given to all the characters and events. The tragic and the gentler pathetic need not be excluded by the tone and treatment. If I could but write one central scene in this vein, all the rest of the Romance would readily arrange itself around that nucleus. The begging-girl would be another American character; the actress too; the caravan people. It must be humorous work, or nothing.

III.

May 12th, Wednesday.—Middleton found his abode here becoming daily more interesting; and he sometimes thought that it was the sympathies with the place and people, buried under the supergrowth of so many ages, but now coming forth with the life and vigor of a fountain, that, long hidden beneath earth and ruins, gushes out singing into the sunshine, as soon as these are removed. He wandered about the neighborhood with insatiable interest; sometimes, and often, lying on a hill-side and gazing at the gray tower of the church; sometimes coming into the village clustered round that same church, and looking at the old timber and plaster houses, the same, except that the thatch had probably been often renewed, that they used to be in his ancestor's days. In those old cottages still dwelt the families, the ——s, the Prices, the Hopnorts, the Copleys, that had dwelt there when America was a scattered progeny of infant colonies; and in the churchyard were the graves of all the generations since—including the dust of those who had seen his ancestor's face before his departure.

The graves, outside the church walls indeed, bore no marks of this antiquity; for it seems not to have been an early practice in England to put stones over such graves; and where it has been done, the climate causes the inscriptions soon to become obliterated and unintelligible. But, within the church, there were rich words of the personages and times with whom Middleton's musings held so much converse.

But one of his greatest employments and pastimes was to ramble through the grounds of Smithell's, making himself as well acquainted with its wood paths, its glens, its woods, its venerable trees, as if he had been bred up there from infancy. Some of those old oaks his ancestor might have been acquainted with, while they were already sturdy and well-grown trees; might have climbed them in boyhood; might have mused beneath them as a lover; might have flung himself at full length on the turf beneath them, in the bitter anguish that must have preceded his departure forever from the home of his forefathers. In order to secure an uninterrupted enjoyment of his rambles here, Middleton had secured the good-will of the game-keepers and other underlings whom he was likely to meet about the grounds, by giving them a shilling or a half-crown; and he was now free to wander where he would, with only the advice rather than the caution, to keep out of the way of their old master,—for there might be trouble, if he should meet a stranger on the grounds, in any of his tantrums. But, in fact, Mr. Eldredge was not much in the habit of walking about the grounds; and there were hours of every day, during which it was altogether improbable that he would have emerged from his own apartments in the manor-house. These were the hours, therefore, when Middleton most frequented the estate; although, to say the truth, he would gladly have so timed his visits as to meet and form an acquaintance with the lonely lord of this beautiful property, his own kinsman, though with so many ages of dark oblivion between. For Middleton had not that feeling of infinite distance in the relationship, which he would have had if his branch of the family had continued in England, and had not intermarried with the other branch, through such a long waste of years; he rather felt as if he were the original emigrant who, long resident on a foreign shore, had now returned, with a heart brimful of tenderness, to revisit the scenes of his youth, and renew his tender relations with those who shared his own blood.

There was not, however, much in what he heard of the character of the present possessor of the estate—or indeed in the strong family characteristic that had become hereditary—to encourage him to attempt any advances. It is very probable that the religion of Mr. Eldredge, as a Catholic, may have excited a prejudice against him, as it certainly had insulated the family, in a great degree, from the sympathies of the neighborhood. Mr. Eldredge, moreover, had resided long on the Continent; long in Italy; and had come back with habits that little accorded with those of the gentry of the neighborhood; so that, in fact, he was almost as much of a stranger, and perhaps quite as little of a real Englishman, as Middleton himself. Be that as it might, Middleton, when he sought to learn something about him, heard the strangest stories of his habits of life, of his temper, and of his employments, from the people with whom he conversed. The old legend, turning upon the monomania of the family, was revived in full force in reference to this poor gentleman; and many a time Middleton's interlocutors shook their wise heads, saying with a knowing look and under their breath that the old gentleman was looking for the track of the Bloody Footstep. They fabled—or said, for it might not have been a false story—that every descendant of this house had a certain portion of his life, during which he sought the track of that footstep which was left on the threshold of the mansion; that he sought it far and wide, over every foot of the estate; not only on the estate, but throughout the neighborhood; not only in the neighborhood but all over England; not only throughout England but all about the world. It was the belief of the neighborhood—at least of some old men and women in it—that the long period of Mr. Eldredge's absence from England had been spent in the search for some trace of those departing footsteps that had never returned. It is very possible—probable, indeed—that there may have been some ground for this remarkable legend; not that it is to be credited that the family of Eldredge, being reckoned among sane men, would seriously have sought, years and generations after the fact, for the first track of those bloody footsteps which the first rain of drippy England must have washed away; to say nothing of the leaves that had fallen and the growth and decay of so many seasons, that covered all traces of them since. But nothing is more probable than that the continual recurrence to the family genealogy, which had been necessitated by the matter of the dormant peerage, had caused the Eldredges, from father to son, to keep alive an interest in that ancestor who had disappeared, and who had been supposed to carry some of the most important family papers with him. But yet it gave Middleton a strange thrill of pleasure, that had something fearful in it, to think that all through these ages he had been waited for, sought for, anxiously expected, as it were; it seemed as if the very ghosts of his kindred, a long shadowy line, held forth their dim arms to welcome him; a line stretching back to the ghosts of those who had flourished in the old, old times; the doubletted and beruffled knightly shades of Queen Elizabeth's time; a long line, stretching from the mediaeval ages, and their duskiness, downward, downward, with only one vacant space, that of him who had left the Bloody Footstep. There was an inexpressible pleasure (airy and evanescent, gone in a moment if he dwelt upon it too thoughtfully, but very sweet) to Middleton's imagination, in this idea. When he reflected, however, that his revelations, if they had any effect at all, might serve only to quench the hopes of these long expectants, it of course made him hesitate to declare himself.

One afternoon, when he was in the midst of musings such as this, he saw at a distance through the park, in the direction of the manor-house, a person who seemed to be walking slowly and seeking for something upon the ground. He was a long way off when Middleton first perceived him; and there were two clumps of trees and underbrush, with interspersed tracts of sunny lawn, between them. The person, whoever he was, kept on, and plunged into the first clump of shrubbery, still keeping his eyes on the ground, as if intensely searching for something. When he emerged from the concealment of the first clump of shrubbery, Middleton saw that he was a tall, thin person, in a dark dress; and this was the chief observation that the distance enabled him to make, as the figure kept slowly onward, in a somewhat wavering line, and plunged into the second clump of shrubbery. From that, too, he emerged; and soon appeared to be a thin elderly figure, of a dark man with gray hair, bent, as it seemed to Middleton, with infirmity, for his figure still stooped even in the intervals when he did not appear to be tracking the ground. But Middleton could not but be surprised at the singular appearance the figure had of setting its foot, at every step, just where a previous footstep had been made, as if he wanted to measure his whole pathway in the track of somebody who had recently gone over the ground in advance of him. Middleton was sitting at the foot of an oak; and he began to feel some awkwardness in the consideration of what he would do if Mr. Eldredge—for he could not doubt that it was he—were to be led just to this spot, in pursuit of his singular occupation. And even so it proved.

Middleton could not feel it manly to fly and hide himself, like a guilty thing; and indeed the hospitality of the English country gentleman in many cases gives the neighborhood and the stranger a certain degree of freedom in the use of the broad expanse of ground in which they and their forefathers have loved to sequester their residences. The figure kept on, showing more and more distinctly the tall, meagre, not unvenerable features of a gentleman in the decline of life, apparently in ill-health; with a dark face, that might once have been full of energy, but now seemed enfeebled by time, passion, and perhaps sorrow. But it was strange to see the earnestness with which he looked on the ground, and the accuracy with which he at last set his foot, apparently adjusting it exactly to some footprint before him; and Middleton doubted not that, having studied and re-studied the family records and the judicial examinations which described exactly the track that was seen the day after the memorable disappearance of his ancestor, Mr. Eldredge was now, in some freak, or for some purpose best known to himself, practically following it out. And follow it out he did, until at last he lifted up his eyes, muttering to himself: "At this point the footsteps wholly disappear."

Lifting his eyes, as we have said, while thus regretfully and despairingly muttering these words, he saw Middleton against the oak, within three paces of him.

May 13th, Thursday.—Mr. Eldredge (for it was he) first kept his eyes fixed full on Middleton's face, with an expression as if he saw him not; but gradually—slowly, at first—he seemed to become aware of his presence; then, with a sudden flush, he took in the idea that he was encountered by a stranger in his secret mood. A flush of anger or shame, perhaps both, reddened over his face; his eyes gleamed; and he spoke hastily and roughly.

"Who are you?" he said. "How come you here? I allow no intruders in my park. Begone, fellow!"

"Really, sir, I did not mean to intrude upon you," said Middleton blandly. "I am aware that I owe you an apology; but the beauties of your park must plead my excuse; and the constant kindness of [the] English gentleman, which admits a stranger to the privilege of enjoying so much of the beauty in which he himself dwells as the stranger's taste permits him to enjoy."

"An artist, perhaps," said Mr. Eldredge, somewhat less uncourteously. "I am told that they love to come here and sketch those old oaks and their vistas, and the old mansion yonder. But you are an intrusive set, you artists, and think that a pencil and a sheet of paper may be your passport anywhere. You are mistaken, sir. My park is not open to strangers."

"I am sorry, then, to have intruded upon you," said Middleton, still in good humor; for in truth he felt a sort of kindness, a sentiment, ridiculous as it may appear, of kindred towards the old gentleman, and besides was not unwilling in any way to prolong a conversation in which he found a singular interest. "I am sorry, especially as I have not even the excuse you kindly suggest for me. I am not an artist, only an American, who have strayed hither to enjoy this gentle, cultivated, tamed nature which I find in English parks, so contrasting with the wild, rugged nature of my native land. I beg your pardon, and will retire."

"An American," repeated Mr. Eldredge, looking curiously at him. "Ah, you are wild men in that country, I suppose, and cannot conceive that an English gentleman encloses his grounds—or that his ancestors have done so before him—for his own pleasure and convenience, and does not calculate on having it infringed upon by everybody, like your own forests, as you say. It is a curious country, that of yours; and in Italy I have seen curious people from it."

"True, sir," said Middleton, smiling. "We send queer specimens abroad; but Englishmen should consider that we spring from them, and that we present after all only a picture of their own characteristics, a little varied by climate and in situation."

Mr. Eldredge looked at him with a certain kind of interest, and it seemed to Middleton that he was not unwilling to continue the conversation, if a fair way to do so could only be offered to him. A secluded man often grasps at any opportunity of communicating with his kind, when it is casually offered to him, and for the nonce is surprisingly familiar, running out towards his chance-companion with the gush of a dammed-up torrent, suddenly unlocked. As Middleton made a motion to retire, he put out his hand with an air of authority to restrain him.

"Stay," said he. "Now that you are here, the mischief is done, and you cannot repair it by hastening away. You have interrupted me in my mood of thought, and must pay the penalty by suggesting other thoughts. I am a lonely man here, having spent most of my life abroad, and am separated from my neighbors by various circumstances. You seem to be an intelligent man. I should like to ask you a few questions about your country."

He looked at Middleton as he spoke, and seemed to be considering in what rank of life he should place him; his dress being such as suited a humble rank. He seemed not to have come to any very certain decision on this point.

"I remember," said he, "you have no distinctions of rank in your country; a convenient thing enough, in some respects. When there are no gentlemen, all are gentlemen. So let it be. You speak of being Englishmen; and it has often occurred to me that Englishmen have left this country and been much missed and sought after, who might perhaps be sought there successfully."

"It is certainly so, Mr. Eldredge," said Middleton, lifting his eyes to his face as he spoke, and then turning them aside. "Many footsteps, the track of which is lost in England, might be found reappearing on the other side of the Atlantic; ay, though it be hundreds of years since the track was lost here."

Middleton, though he had refrained from looking full at Mr. Eldredge as he spoke, was conscious that he gave a great start; and he remained silent for a moment or two, and when he spoke there was the tremor in his voice of a nerve that had been struck and still vibrated.

"That is a singular idea of yours," he at length said; "not singular in itself, but strangely coincident with something that happened to be occupying my mind. Have you ever heard any such instances as you speak of?"

"Yes," replied Middleton. "I have had pointed out to me the rightful heir to a Scottish earldom, in the person of an American farmer, in his shirt-sleeves. There are many Americans who believe themselves to hold similar claims. And I have known one family, at least, who had in their possession, and had had for two centuries, a secret that might have been worth wealth and honors if known in England. Indeed, being kindred as we are, it cannot but be the case."

Mr. Eldredge appeared to be much struck by these last words, and gazed wistfully, almost wildly, at Middleton, as if debating with himself whether to say more. He made a step or two aside; then returned abruptly, and spoke.

"Can you tell me the name of the family in which this secret was kept?" said he; "and the nature of the secret?"

"The nature of the secret," said Middleton, smiling, "was not likely to be extended to any one out of the family. The name borne by the family was Middleton. There is no member of it, so far as I am aware, at this moment remaining in America."

"And has the secret died with them?" asked Mr. Eldredge.

"They communicated it to none," said Middleton.

"It is a pity! It was a villainous wrong," said Mr. Eldredge. "And so, it may be, some ancient line, in the old country, is defrauded of its rights for want of what might have been obtained from this Yankee, whose democracy has demoralized them to the perception of what is due to the antiquity of descent, and of the bounden duty that there is, in all ranks, to keep up the honor of a family that has had potence enough to preserve itself in distinction for a thousand years."

"Yes," said Middleton, quietly, "we have sympathy with what is strong and vivacious to-day; none with what was so yesterday."

The remark seemed not to please Mr. Eldredge; he frowned, and muttered something to himself; but recovering himself, addressed Middleton with more courtesy than at the commencement of their interview; and, with this graciousness, his face and manner grew very agreeable, almost fascinating: he [was] still haughty, however.

"Well, sir," said he, "I am not sorry to have met you. I am a solitary man, as I have said, and a little communication with a stranger is a refreshment, which I enjoy seldom enough to be sensible of it. Pray, are you staying hereabouts?"

Middleton signified to him that he might probably spend some little time in the village.

"Then, during your stay," said Mr. Eldredge, "make free use of the walks in these grounds; and though it is not probable that you will meet me in them again, you need apprehend no second questioning of your right to be here. My house has many points of curiosity that may be of interest to a stranger from a new country. Perhaps you have heard of some of them."

"I have heard some wild legend about a Bloody Footstep," answered Middleton; "indeed, I think I remember hearing something about it in my own country; and having a fanciful sort of interest in such things, I took advantage of the hospitable custom which opens the doors of curious old houses to strangers, to go to see it. It seemed to me, I confess, only a natural stain in the old stone that forms the doorstep."

"There, sir," said Mr. Eldredge, "let me say that you came to a very foolish conclusion; and so, good-by, sir."

And without further ceremony, he cast an angry glance at Middleton, who perceived that the old gentleman reckoned the Bloody Footstep among his ancestral honors, and would probably have parted with his claim to the peerage almost as soon as have given up the legend.

Present aspect of the story: Middleton on his arrival becomes acquainted with the old Hospitaller, and is familiarized at the Hospital. He pays a visit in his company to the manor-house, but merely glimpses at its remarkable things, at this visit, among others at the old cabinet, which does not, at first view, strike him very strongly. But, on musing about his visit afterwards, he finds the recollection of the cabinet strangely identifying itself with his previous imaginary picture of the palatial mansion; so that at last he begins to conceive the mistake he has made. At this first [visit], he does not have a personal interview with the possessor of the estate; but, as the Hospitaller and himself go from room to room, he finds that the owner is preceding them, shyly flitting like a ghost, so as to avoid them. Then there is a chapter about the character of the Eldredge of the day, a Catholic, a morbid, shy man, representing all the peculiarities of an old family, and generally thought to be insane. And then comes the interview between him and Middleton, where the latter excites such an interest that he dwells upon the old man's mind, and the latter probably takes pains to obtain further intercourse with him, and perhaps invites him to dinner, and [to] spend a night in his house.

If so, this second meeting must lead to the examination of the cabinet, and the discovery of some family documents in it. Perhaps the cabinet may be in Middleton's sleeping-chamber, and he examines it by himself, before going to bed; and finds out a secret which will perplex him how to deal with it.

May 14th, Friday.—We have spoken several times already of a young girl, who was seen at this period about the little antiquated village of Smithells; a girl in manners and in aspect unlike those of the cottages amid which she dwelt. Middleton had now so often met her, and in solitary places, that an acquaintance had inevitably established itself between them. He had ascertained that she had lodgings at a farm-house near by, and that she was connected in some way with the old Hospitaller, whose acquaintance had proved of such interest to him; but more than this he could not learn either from her or others. But he was greatly attracted and interested by the free spirit and fearlessness of this young woman; nor could he conceive where, in staid and formal England, she had grown up to be such as she was, so without manner, so without art, yet so capable of doing and thinking for herself. She had no reserve, apparently, yet never seemed to sin against decorum; it never appeared to restrain her that anything she might wish to do was contrary to custom; she had nothing of what could be called shyness in her intercourse with him; and yet he was conscious of an unapproachableness in Alice. Often, in the old man's presence, she mingled in the conversation that went on between him and Middleton, and with an acuteness that betokened a sphere of thought much beyond what could be customary with young English maidens; and Middleton was often reminded of the theories of those in our own country, who believe that the amelioration of society depends greatly on the part that women shall hereafter take, according to their individual capacity, in all the various pursuits of life. These deeper thoughts, these higher qualities, surprised him as they showed themselves, whenever occasion called them forth, under the light, gay, and frivolous exterior which she had at first seemed to present. Middleton often amused himself with surmises in what rank of life Alice could have been bred, being so free of all conventional rule, yet so nice and delicate in her perception of the true proprieties that she never shocked him.

One morning, when they had met in one of Middleton's rambles about the neighborhood, they began to talk of America; and Middleton described to Alice the stir that was being made in behalf of women's rights; and he said that whatever cause was generous and disinterested always, in that country, derived much of its power from the sympathy of women, and that the advocates of every such cause were in favor of yielding the whole field of human effort to be shared with women.

"I have been surprised," said he, "in the little I have seen and heard of English women, to discover what a difference there is between them and my own countrywomen."

"I have heard," said Alice, with a smile, "that your countrywomen are a far more delicate and fragile race than Englishwomen; pale, feeble hot-house plants, unfit for the wear and tear of life, without energy of character, or any slightest degree of physical strength to base it upon. If, now, you had these large-framed Englishwomen, you might, I should imagine, with better hopes, set about changing the system of society, so as to allow them to struggle in the strife of politics, or any other strife, hand to hand, or side by side with men."

"If any countryman of mine has said this of our women," exclaimed Middleton, indignantly, "he is a slanderous villain, unworthy to have been borne by an American mother; if an Englishman has said it—as I know many of them have and do—let it pass as one of the many prejudices only half believed, with which they strive to console themselves for the inevitable sense that the American race is destined to higher purposes than their own. But pardon me; I forgot that I was speaking to an Englishwoman, for indeed you do not remind me of them. But, I assure you, the world has not seen such women as make up, I had almost said the mass of womanhood in my own country; slight in aspect, slender in frame, as you suggest, but yet capable of bringing forth stalwart men; they themselves being of inexhaustible courage, patience, energy; soft and tender, deep of heart, but high of purpose. Gentle, refined, but bold in every good cause."

"Oh, yea have said quite enough," replied Alice, who had seemed ready to laugh outright, during this encomium. "I think I see one of these paragons now, in a Bloomer, I think you call it, swaggering along with a Bowie knife at her girdle, smoking a cigar, no doubt, and tippling sherry-cobblers and mint-juleps. It must be a pleasant life."

"I should think you, at least, might form a more just idea of what women become," said Middleton, considerably piqued, "in a country where the rules of conventionalism are somewhat relaxed; where woman, whatever you may think, is far more profoundly educated than in England, where a few ill-taught accomplishments, a little geography, a catechism of science, make up the sum, under the superintendence of a governess; the mind being kept entirely inert as to any capacity for thought. They are cowards, except within certain rules and forms; they spend a life of old proprieties, and die, and if their souls do not die with them, it is Heaven's mercy."

Alice did not appear in the least moved to anger, though considerably to mirth, by this description of the character of English females. She laughed as she replied, "I see there is little danger of your leaving your heart in England." She added more seriously, "And permit me to say, I trust, Mr. Middleton, that you remain as much American in other respects as in your preference of your own race of women. The American who comes hither and persuades himself that he is one with Englishmen, it seems to me, makes a great mistake; at least, if he is correct in such an idea he is not worthy of his own country, and the high development that awaits it. There is much that is seductive in our life, but I think it is not upon the higher impulses of our nature that such seductions act. I should think ill of the American who, for any causes of ambition,—any hope of wealth or rank,—or even for the sake of any of those old, delightful ideas of the past, the associations of ancestry, the loveliness of an age-long home,—the old poetry and romance that haunt these ancient villages and estates of England,—would give up the chance of acting upon the unmoulded future of America."

"And you, an Englishwoman, speak thus!" exclaimed Middleton. "You perhaps speak truly; and it may be that your words go to a point where they are especially applicable at this moment. But where have you learned these ideas? And how is it that you know how to awake these sympathies, that have slept perhaps too long?"

"Think only if what I have said be truth," replied Alice. "It is no matter who or what I am that speak it."

"Do you speak," asked Middleton, from a sudden impulse, "with any secret knowledge affecting a matter now in my mind?"

Alice shook her head, as she turned away; but Middleton could not determine whether the gesture was meant as a negative to his question, or merely as declining to answer it. She left him; and he found himself strangely disturbed with thoughts of his own country, of the life that he ought to be leading there, the struggles in which he ought to be taking part; and, with these motives in his impressible mind, the motives that had hitherto kept him in England seemed unworthy to influence him.

May 15th, Saturday.—It was not long after Middleton's meeting with Mr. Eldredge in the park of Smithells, that he received—what it is precisely the most common thing to receive—an invitation to dine at the manor-house and spend the night. The note was written with much appearance of cordiality, as well as in a respectful style; and Middleton could not but perceive that Mr. Eldredge must have been making some inquiries as to his social status, in order to feel him justified in putting him on this footing of equality. He had no hesitation in accepting the invitation, and on the appointed day was received in the old house of his forefathers as a guest. The owner met him, not quite on the frank and friendly footing expressed in his note, but still with a perfect and polished courtesy, which however could not hide from the sensitive Middleton a certain coldness, a something that seemed to him Italian rather than English; a symbol of a condition of things between them, undecided, suspicious, doubtful very likely. Middleton's own manner corresponded to that of his host, and they made few advances towards more intimate acquaintance. Middleton was however recompensed for his host's unapproachableness by the society of his daughter, a young lady born indeed in Italy, but who had been educated in a Catholic family in England; so that here was another relation—the first female one—to whom he had been introduced. She was a quiet, shy, undemonstrative young woman, with a fine bloom and other charms which she kept as much in the background as possible, with maiden reserve. (There is a Catholic priest at table.)

Mr. Eldredge talked chiefly, during dinner, of art, with which his long residence in Italy had made him thoroughly acquainted, and for which he seemed to have a genuine taste and enjoyment. It was a subject on which Middleton knew little; but he felt the interest in it which appears to be not uncharacteristic of Americans, among the earliest of their developments of cultivation; nor had he failed to use such few opportunities as the English public or private galleries offered him to acquire the rudiments of a taste. He was surprised at the depth of some of Mr. Eldredge's remarks on the topics thus brought up, and at the sensibility which appeared to be disclosed by his delicate appreciation of some of the excellences of those great masters who wrote their epics, their tender sonnets, or their simple ballads, upon canvas; and Middleton conceived a respect for him which he had not hitherto felt, and which possibly Mr. Eldredge did not quite deserve. Taste seems to be a department of moral sense; and yet it is so little identical with it, and so little implies conscience, that some of the worst men in the world have been the most refined.

After Miss Eldredge had retired, the host appeared to desire to make the dinner a little more social than it had hitherto been; he called for a peculiar species of wine from Southern Italy, which he said was the most delicious production of the grape, and had very seldom, if ever before been imported pure into England. A delicious perfume came from the cradled bottle, and bore an ethereal, evanescent testimony to the truth of what he said: and the taste, though too delicate for wine quaffed in England, was nevertheless delicious, when minutely dwelt upon.

"It gives me pleasure to drink your health, Mr. Middleton," said the host. "We might well meet as friends in England, for I am hardly more an Englishman than yourself; bred up, as I have been, in Italy, and coming back hither at my age, unaccustomed to the manners of the country, with few friends, and insulated from society by a faith which makes most people regard me as an enemy. I seldom welcome people here, Mr. Middleton; but you are welcome."

"I thank you, Mr. Eldredge, and may fairly say that the circumstances to which you allude make me accept your hospitality with a warmer feeling than

I otherwise might. Strangers, meeting in a strange land, have a sort of tie in their foreignness to those around them, though there be no positive relation between themselves."

"We are friends, then?" said Mr. Eldredge, looking keenly at Middleton, as if to discover exactly how much was meant by the compact. He continued, "You know, I suppose, Mr. Middleton, the situation in which I find myself on returning to my hereditary estate, which has devolved to me somewhat unexpectedly by the death of a younger man than myself. There is an old flaw here, as perhaps you have been told, which keeps me out of a property long kept in the guardianship of the crown, and of a barony, one of the oldest in England. There is an idea—a tradition—a legend, founded, however, on evidence of some weight, that there is still in existence the possibility of finding the proof which we need, to confirm our cause."

"I am most happy to hear it, Mr. Eldredge," said Middleton.

"But," continued his host, "I am bound to remember and to consider that for several generations there seems to have been the same idea, and the same expectation; whereas nothing has ever come of it. Now, among other suppositions—perhaps wild ones—it has occurred to me that this testimony, the desirable proof, may exist on your side of the Atlantic; for it has long enough been sought here in vain."

"As I said in our meeting in your park, Mr. Eldredge," replied Middleton, "such a suggestion may very possibly be true; yet let me point out that the long lapse of years, and the continual melting and dissolving of family institutions—the consequent scattering of family documents, and the annihilation of traditions from memory, all conspire against its probability."

"And yet, Mr. Middleton," said his host, "when we talked together at our first singular interview, you made use of an expression—of one remarkable phrase—which dwelt upon my memory and now recurs to it."

"And what was that, Mr. Eldredge?" asked Middleton.

"You spoke," replied his host, "of the Bloody Footstep reappearing on the threshold of the old palace of S———. Now where, let me ask you, did you ever hear this strange name, which you then spoke, and which I have since spoken?"

"From my father's lips, when a child, in America," responded Middleton.

"It is very strange," said Mr. Eldredge, in a hasty, dissatisfied tone.

"I do not see my way through this."

May 16, Sunday.—Middleton had been put into a chamber in the oldest part of the house, the furniture of which was of antique splendor, well befitting to have come down for ages, well befitting the hospitality shown to noble and even royal guests. It was the same room in which, at his first visit to the house, Middleton's attention had been drawn to the cabinet, which he had subsequently remembered as the palatial residence in which he had harbored so many dreams. It still stood in the chamber, making the principal object in it, indeed; and when Middleton was left alone, he contemplated it not without a certain awe, which at the same time he felt to be ridiculous. He advanced towards it, and stood contemplating the mimic façade, wondering at the singular fact of this piece of furniture having been preserved in traditionary history, when so much had been forgotten,—when even the features and architectural characteristics of the mansion in which it was merely a piece of furniture had been forgotten. And, as he gazed at it, he half thought himself an actor in a fairy portal [tale?]; and would not have been surprised—at least, he would have taken it with the composure of a dream—if the mimic portal had unclosed, and a form of pigmy majesty had appeared within, beckoning him to enter and find the revelation of what had so long perplexed him. The key of the cabinet was in the lock, and knowing that it was not now the receptacle of anything in the shape of family papers, he threw it open; and there appeared the mosaic floor, the representation of a stately, pillared hall, with the doors on either side, opening, as would seem, into various apartments. And here should have stood the visionary figures of his ancestry, waiting to welcome the descendant of their race, who had so long delayed his coming. After looking and musing a considerable time,—even till the old clock from the turret of the house told twelve, he turned away with a sigh, and went to bed. The wind moaned through the ancestral trees; the old house creaked as with ghostly footsteps; the curtains of his bed seemed to waver. He was now at home; yes, he had found his home, and was sheltered at last under the ancestral roof after all those long, long wanderings,—after the little log-built hut of the early settlement, after the straight roof of the American house, after all the many roofs of two hundred years, here he was at last under the one which he had left, on that fatal night, when the Bloody Footstep was so mysteriously impressed on the threshold. As he drew nearer and nearer towards sleep, it seemed more and more to him as if he were the very individual—the self-same one throughout the whole—who had done, seen, suffered, all these long toils and vicissitudes, and were now come back to rest, and found his weariness so great that there could be no rest.

Nevertheless, he did sleep; and it may be that his dreams went on, and grew vivid, and perhaps became truer in proportion to their vividness. When he awoke he had a perception, an intuition, that he had been dreaming about the cabinet, which, in his sleeping imagination, had again assumed the magnitude and proportions of a stately mansion, even as he had seen it afar from the other side of the Atlantic. Some dim associations remained lingering behind, the dying shadows of very vivid ones which had just filled his mind; but as he looked at the cabinet, there was some idea that still seemed to come so near his consciousness that, every moment, he felt on the point of grasping it. During the process of dressing, he still kept his eyes turned involuntarily towards the cabinet, and at last he approached it, and looked within the mimic portal, still endeavoring to recollect what it was that he had heard or dreamed about it,—what half obliterated remembrance from childhood, what fragmentary last night's dream it was, that thus haunted him. It must have been some association of one or the other nature that led him to press his finger on one particular square of the mosaic pavement; and as he did so, the thin plate of polished marble slipt aside. It disclosed, indeed, no hollow receptacle, but only another leaf of marble, in the midst of which appeared to be a key-hole: to this Middleton applied the little antique key to which we have several times alluded, and found it fit precisely. The instant it was turned, the whole mimic floor of the hall rose, by the action of a secret spring, and discovered a shallow recess beneath. Middleton looked eagerly in, and saw that it contained documents, with antique seals of wax appended; he took but one glance at them, and closed the receptacle as it was before.

Why did he do so? He felt that there would be a meanness and wrong in inspecting these family papers, coming to the knowledge of them, as he had, through the opportunities offered by the hospitality of the owner of the estate; nor, on the other hand, did he feel such confidence in his host, as to make him willing to trust these papers in his hands, with any certainty that they would be put to an honorable use. The case was one demanding consideration, and he put a strong curb upon his impatient curiosity, conscious that, at all events, his first impulsive feeling was that he ought not to examine these papers without the presence of his host or some other authorized witness. Had he exercised any casuistry about the point, however, he might have argued that these papers, according to all appearance, dated from a period to which his own hereditary claims ascended, and to circumstances in which his own rightful interest was as strong as that of Mr. Eldredge. But he had acted on his first impulse, closed the secret receptacle, and hastening his toilet descended from his room; and, it being still too early for breakfast, resolved to ramble about the immediate vicinity of the house. As he passed the little chapel, he heard within the voice of the priest performing mass, and felt how strange was this sign of mediaeval religion and foreign manners in homely England.

As the story looks now: Eldredge, bred, and perhaps born, in Italy, and a Catholic, with views to the church before he inherited the estate, has not the English moral sense and simple honor; can scarcely be called an Englishman at all. Dark suspicions of past crime, and of the possibility of future crime, may be thrown around him; an atmosphere of doubt shall envelop him, though, as regards manners, he may be highly refined. Middleton shall find in the house a priest; and at his first visit he shall have seen a small chapel, adorned with the richness, as to marbles, pictures, and frescoes, of those that we see in the churches at Rome; and here the Catholic forms of worship shall be kept up. Eldredge shall have had an Italian mother, and shall have the personal characteristics of an Italian. There shall be something sinister about him, the more apparent when Middleton's visit draws to a conclusion; and the latter shall feel convinced that they part in enmity, so far as Eldredge is concerned. He shall not speak of his discovery in the cabinet.

May 17th, Monday.—Unquestionably, the appointment of Middleton as minister to one of the minor Continental courts must take place in the interval between Eldredge's meeting him in the park, and his inviting him to his house. After Middleton's appointment, the two encounter each other at the Mayor's dinner in St. Mary's Hall, and Eldredge, startled at meeting the vagrant, as he deemed him, under such a character, remembers the hints of some secret knowledge of the family history, which Middleton had thrown out. He endeavors, both in person and by the priest, to make out what Middleton really is, and what he knows, and what he intends; but Middleton is on his guard, yet cannot help arousing Eldredge's suspicions that he has views upon the estate and title. It is possible, too, that Middleton may have come to the knowledge—may have had some knowledge—of some shameful or criminal fact connected with Mr. Eldredge's life on the Continent; the old Hospitaller, possibly, may have told him this, from some secret malignity hereafter to be accounted for. Supposing Eldredge to attempt his murder, by poison for instance, bringing back into modern life his old hereditary Italian plots; and into English life a sort of crime which does not belong to it,—which did not, at least, although at this very period there have been fresh and numerous instances of it. There might be a scene in which Middleton and Eldredge come to a fierce and bitter explanation; for in Eldredge's character there must be the English surly boldness as well as the Italian subtlety; and here, Middleton shall tell him what he knows of his past character and life, and also what he knows of his own hereditary claims. Eldredge might have committed a murder in Italy; might have been a patriot, and betrayed his friends to death for a bribe, bearing another name than his own in Italy; indeed, he might have joined them only as an informer. All this he had tried to sink, when he came to England in the character of a gentleman of ancient name and large estate. But this infamy of his previous character must be foreboded from the first by the manner in which Eldredge is introduced; and it must make his evil designs on Middleton appear natural and probable. It may be, that Middleton has learned Eldredge's previous character, through some Italian patriot who had taken refuge in America, and there become intimate with him; and it should be a piece of secret history, not known to the world in general, so that Middleton might seem to Eldredge the sole depositary of the secret then in England. He feels a necessity of getting rid of him; and thenceforth Middleton's path lies always among pitfalls; indeed, the first attempt should follow promptly and immediately on his rupture with Eldredge. The utmost pains must be taken with this incident to give it an air of reality; or else it must be quite removed out of the sphere of reality by an intensified atmosphere of romance. I think the old Hospitaller must interfere to prevent the success of this attempt, perhaps through the means of Alice.

The result of Eldredge's criminal and treacherous designs is, somehow or other, that he comes to his death; and Middleton and Alice are left to administer on the remains of the story; perhaps, the Mayor being his friend, he may be brought into play here. The foreign ecclesiastic shall likewise come forward, and he shall prove to be a man of subtile policy perhaps, yet a man of religion and honor; with a Jesuit's principles, but a Jesuit's devotion and self-sacrifice. The old Hospitaller must die in his bed, or some other how; or perhaps not—we shall see. He may just as well be left in the Hospital. Eldredge's attempt on Middleton must be in some way peculiar to Italy, and which he shall have learned there; and, by the way, at his dinner-table there shall be a Venice glass, one of the kind that were supposed to be shattered when poison was put into them. When Eldredge produces his rare wine, he shall pour it into this, with a jesting allusion to the legend. Perhaps the mode of Eldredge's attempt on Middleton's life shall be a reproduction of the attempt made two hundred years before; and Middleton's knowledge of that incident shall be the means of his salvation. That would be a good idea; in fact, I think it must be done so and no otherwise. It is not to be forgotten that there is a taint of insanity in Eldredge's blood, accounting for much that is wild and absurd, at the same time that it must be subtile, in his conduct; one of those perplexing mad people, whose lunacy you are continually mistaking for wickedness or vice versa. This shall be the priest's explanation and apology for him, after his death. I wish I could get hold of the Newgate Calendar, the older volumes, or any other book of murders—the Causes Celébrès, for instance. The legendary murder, or attempt at it, will bring its own imaginative probability with it, when repeated by Eldredge; and at the same time it will have a dreamlike effect; so that Middleton shall hardly know whether he is awake or not. This incident is very essential towards bringing together the past time and the present, and the two ends of the story.

May 18th, Tuesday.—All down through the ages since Edward had disappeared from home, leaving that bloody footstep on the threshold, there had been legends and strange stories of the murder and the manner of it. These legends differed very much among themselves. According to some, his brother had awaited him there, and stabbed him on the threshold. According to others, he had been murdered in his chamber, and dragged out. A third story told, that he was escaping with his lady love, when they were overtaken on the threshold, and the young man slain. It was impossible at this distance of time to ascertain which of these legends was the true one, or whether either of them had any portion of truth, further than that the young man had actually disappeared from that night, and that it never was certainly known to the public that any intelligence had ever afterwards been received from him. Now, Middleton may have communicated to Eldredge the truth in regard to the matter; as, for instance, that he had stabbed him with a certain dagger that was still kept among the curiosities of the manor-house. Of course, that will not do. It must be some very ingenious and artificially natural thing, an artistic affair in its way, that should strike the fancy of such a man as Eldredge, and appear to him altogether fit, mutatis mutandis, to be applied to his own requirements and purposes. I do not at present see in the least how this is to be wrought out. There shall be everything to make Eldredge look with the utmost horror and alarm at any chance that he may be superseded and ousted from his possession of the estate; for he shall only recently have established his claim to it, tracing out his pedigree, when the family was supposed to be extinct. And he is come to these comfortable quarters after a life of poverty, uncertainty, difficulty, hanging loose on society; and therefore he shall be willing to risk soul and body both, rather than return to his former state. Perhaps his daughter shall be introduced as a young Italian girl, to whom Middleton shall decide to leave the estate.

On the failure of his design, Eldredge may commit suicide, and be found dead in the wood; at any rate, some suitable end shall be contrived, adapted to his wants. This character must not be so represented as to shut him out completely from the reader's sympathies; he shall have taste, sentiment, even a capacity for affection, nor, I think, ought he to have any hatred or bitter feeling against the man whom he resolves to murder. In the closing scenes, when he thinks the fate of Middleton approaching, there might even be a certain tenderness towards him, a desire to make the last drops of life delightful; if well done, this would produce a certain sort of horror, that I do not remember to have seen effected in literature. Possibly the ancient emigrant might be supposed to have fallen into an ancient mine, down a precipice, into some pitfall; no, not so. Into a river; into a moat. As Middleton's pretensions to birth are not publicly known, there will be no reason why, at his sudden death, suspicion should fix on Eldredge as the murderer; and it shall be his object so to contrive his death as that it shall appear the result of accident. Having failed in effecting Middleton's death by this excellent way, he shall perhaps think that he cannot do better than to make his own exit in precisely the same manner. It might be easy, and as delightful as any death could be; no ugliness in it, no blood; for the Bloody Footstep of old times might be the result of the failure of the old plot, not of its success. Poison seems to be the only elegant method; but poison is vulgar, and in many respects unfit for my purpose. It won't do. Whatever it may be, it must not come upon the reader as a sudden and new thing, but as one that might have been foreseen from afar, though he shall not actually have foreseen it until it is about to happen. It must be prevented through the agency of Alice. Alice may have been an artist in Rome, and there have known Eldredge and his daughter, and thus she may have become their guest in England; or he may be patronizing her now—at all events she shall be the friend of the daughter, and shall have a just appreciation of the father's character. It shall be partly due to her high counsel that Middleton foregoes his claim to the estate, and prefers the life of an American, with its lofty possibilities for himself and his race, to the position of an Englishman of property and title; and she, for her part, shall choose the condition and prospects of woman in America, to the emptiness of the life of a woman of rank in England. So they shall depart, lofty and poor, out of the home which might be their own, if they would stoop to make it so. Possibly the daughter of Eldredge may be a girl not yet in her teens, for whom Alice has the affection of an elder sister.

It should be a very carefully and highly wrought scene, occurring just before Eldredge's actual attempt on Middleton's life, in which all the brilliancy of his character—which shall before have gleamed upon the reader—shall come out, with pathos, with wit, with insight, with knowledge of life. Middleton shall be inspired by this, and shall vie with him in exhilaration of spirits; but the ecclesiastic shall look on with singular attention, and some appearance of alarm; and the suspicion of Alice shall likewise be aroused. The old Hospitaller may have gained his situation partly by proving himself a man of the neighborhood, by right of descent; so that he, too, shall have a hereditary claim to be in the Romance.

Eldredge's own position as a foreigner in the midst of English home life, insulated and dreary, shall represent to Middleton, in some degree, what his own would be, were he to accept the estate. But Middleton shall not come to the decision to resign it, without having to repress a deep yearning for that sense of long, long rest in an age-consecrated home, which he had felt so deeply to be the happy lot of Englishmen. But this ought to be rejected, as not belonging to his country, nor to the age, nor any longer possible.

May 19th, Wednesday.—The connection of the old Hospitaller with the story is not at all clear. He is an American by birth, but deriving his English origin from the neighborhood of the Hospital, where he has finally established himself. Some one of his ancestors may have been somehow connected with the ancient portion of the story. He has been a friend of Middleton's father, who reposed entire confidence in him, trusting him with all his fortune, which the Hospitaller risked in his enormous speculations, and lost it all. His fame had been great in the financial world. There were circumstances that made it dangerous for his whereabouts to be known, and so he had come hither and found refuge in this institution, where Middleton finds him, but does not know who he is. In the vacancy of a mind formerly so active, he has taken to the study of local antiquities; and from his former intimacy with Middleton's father, he has a knowledge of the American part of the story, which he connects with the English portion, disclosed by his researches here; so that he is quite aware that Middleton has claims to the estate, which might be urged successfully against the present possessor. He is kindly disposed towards the son of his friend, whom he had so greatly injured; but he is now very old, and——. Middleton has been directed to this old man by a friend in America, as one likely to afford him all possible assistance in his researches; and so he seeks him out and forms an acquaintance with him, which the old man encourages to a certain extent, taking an evident interest in him, but does not disclose himself; nor does Middleton suspect him to be an American. The characteristic life of the Hospital is brought out, and the individual character of this old man, vegetating here after an active career, melancholy and miserable; sometimes torpid with the slow approach of utmost age; sometimes feeble, peevish, wavering; sometimes shining out with a wisdom resulting from originally bright faculties, ripened by experience. The character must not be allowed to get vague, but, with gleams of romance, must yet be kept homely and natural by little touches of his daily life.

As for Alice, I see no necessity for her being anywise related to or connected with the old Hospitaller. As originally conceived, I think she may be an artist—a sculptress—whom Eldredge had known in Rome. No; she might be a granddaughter of the old Hospitaller, born and bred in America, but who had resided two or three years in Rome in the study of her art, and have there acquired a knowledge of the Eldredges and have become fond of the little Italian girl his daughter. She has lodgings in the village, and of course is often at the Hospital, and often at the Hall; she makes busts and little statues, and is free, wild, tender, proud, domestic, strange, natural, artistic; and has at bottom the characteristics of the American woman, with the principles of the strong-minded sect; and Middleton shall be continually puzzled at meeting such a phenomenon in England. By and by, the internal influence [evidence?] of her sentiments (though there shall be nothing to confirm it in her manner) shall lead him to charge her with being an American.

Now, as to the arrangement of the Romance;—it begins as an integral and essential part, with my introduction, giving a pleasant and familiar summary of my life in the Consulate at Liverpool; the strange species of Americans, with strange purposes, in England, whom I used to meet there; and, especially, how my countrymen used to be put out of their senses by the idea of inheritances of English property. Then I shall particularly instance one gentleman who called on me on first coming over; a description of him must be given, with touches that shall puzzle the reader to decide whether it is not an actual portrait. And then this Romance shall be offered, half seriously, as the account of the fortunes that he met with in his search for his hereditary home. Enough of his ancestral story may be given to explain what is to follow in the Romance; or perhaps this may be left to the scenes of his intercourse with the old Hospitaller.

The Romance proper opens with Middleton's arrival at what he has reason to think is the neighborhood of his ancestral home, and here he makes application to the old Hospitaller. Middleton shall be described as approaching the Hospital, which shall be pretty literally copied after Leicester's, although the surrounding village must be on a much smaller scale of course. Much elaborateness may be given to this portion of the book. Middleton shall have assumed a plain dress, and shall seek to make no acquaintances except that of the old Hospitaller; the acquaintance of Alice naturally following. The old Hospitaller and he go together to the old Hall, where, as they pass through the rooms, they find that the proprietor is flitting like a ghost before them from chamber to chamber; they catch his reflection in a glass, &c., &c. When these have been wrought up sufficiently, shall come the scene in the wood, where Eldredge is seen yielding to the superstition that he has inherited, respecting the old secret of the family, on the discovery of which depends the enforcement of his claim to a title. All this while, Middleton has appeared in the character of a man of no note; and now, through some political change, not necessarily told, he receives a packet addressed to him as an ambassador, and containing a notice of his appointment to that dignity. A paragraph in the "Times" confirms the fact, and makes it known in the neighborhood. Middleton immediately becomes an object of attention; the gentry call upon him; the Mayor of the neighboring county-town invites him to dinner, which shall be described with all its antique formalities. Here he meets Eldredge, who is surprised, remembering the encounter in the wood; but passes it all off, like a man of the world, makes his acquaintance, and invites him to the Hall. Perhaps he may make a visit of some time here, and become intimate, to a certain degree, with all parties; and here things shall ripen themselves for Eldredge's attempt upon his life.

About Author

Nathaniel Hawthorne (**Hathorne**; July 4, 1804 – May 19, 1864) was an American novelist, dark romantic, and short story writer. His works often focus on history, morality, and religion.

He was born in 1804 in Salem, Massachusetts, to Nathaniel Hathorne and the former Elizabeth Clarke Manning. His ancestors include John Hathorne, the only judge involved in the Salem witch trials who never repented of his actions. He entered Bowdoin College in 1821, was elected to Phi Beta Kappa in 1824, and graduated in 1825. He published his first work in 1828, the novel Fanshawe; he later tried to suppress it, feeling that it was not equal to the standard of his later work. He published several short stories in periodicals, which he collected in 1837 as Twice-Told Tales. The next year, he became engaged to Sophia Peabody. He worked at the Boston Custom House and joined Brook Farm, a transcendentalist community, before marrying Peabody in 1842. The couple moved to The Old Manse in Concord, Massachusetts, later moving to Salem, the Berkshires, then to The Wayside in Concord. The Scarlet Letter was published in 1850, followed by a succession of other novels. A political appointment as consul took Hawthorne and family to Europe before their return to Concord in 1860. Hawthorne died on May 19, 1864, and was survived by his wife and their three children.

Much of Hawthorne's writing centers on New England, many works featuring moral metaphors with an anti-Puritan inspiration. His fiction works are considered part of the Romantic movement and, more specifically, dark romanticism. His themes often center on the inherent evil and sin of humanity, and his works often have moral messages and deep psychological complexity. His published works include novels, short stories, and a biography of his college friend Franklin Pierce, the 14th President of the United States.

Biography

Early life

Nathaniel Hawthorne was born on July 4, 1804, in Salem, Massachusetts;

his birthplace is preserved and open to the public. William Hathorne was the author's great-great-great-grandfather. He was a Puritan and was the first of the family to emigrate from England, settling in Dorchester, Massachusetts, before moving to Salem. There he became an important member of the Massachusetts Bay Colony and held many political positions, including magistrate and judge, becoming infamous for his harsh sentencing. William's son and the author's great-great-grandfather John Hathorne was one of the judges who oversaw the Salem witch trials. Hawthorne probably added the "w" to his surname in his early twenties, shortly after graduating from college, in an effort to dissociate himself from his notorious forebears. Hawthorne's father Nathaniel Hathorne Sr. was a sea captain who died in 1808 of yellow fever in Suriname; he had been a member of the East India Marine Society. After his death, his widow moved with young Nathaniel and two daughters to live with relatives named the Mannings in Salem, where they lived for 10 years. Young Hawthorne was hit on the leg while playing "bat and ball" on November 10, 1813, and he became lame and bedridden for a year, though several physicians could find nothing wrong with him.

In the summer of 1816, the family lived as boarders with farmers before moving to a home recently built specifically for them by Hawthorne's uncles Richard and Robert Manning in Raymond, Maine, near Sebago Lake. Years later, Hawthorne looked back at his time in Maine fondly: "Those were delightful days, for that part of the country was wild then, with only scattered clearings, and nine tenths of it primeval woods." In 1819, he was sent back to Salem for school and soon complained of homesickness and being too far from his mother and sisters. He distributed seven issues of The Spectator to his family in August and September 1820 for the sake of having fun. The homemade newspaper was written by hand and included essays, poems, and news featuring the young author's adolescent humor.

Hawthorne's uncle Robert Manning insisted that the boy attend college, despite Hawthorne's protests. With the financial support of his uncle, Hawthorne was sent to Bowdoin College in 1821, partly because of family connections in the area, and also because of its relatively inexpensive tuition rate. Hawthorne met future president Franklin Pierce on the way to

Bowdoin, at the stage stop in Portland, and the two became fast friends. Once at the school, he also met future poet Henry Wadsworth Longfellow, future congressman Jonathan Cilley, and future naval reformer Horatio Bridge. He graduated with the class of 1825, and later described his college experience to Richard Henry Stoddard:

> I was educated (as the phrase is) at Bowdoin College. I was an idle student, negligent of college rules and the Procrustean details of academic life, rather choosing to nurse my own fancies than to dig into Greek roots and be numbered among the learned Thebans.

Early career

In 1836, Hawthorne served as the editor of the American Magazine of Useful and Entertaining Knowledge. At the time, he boarded with poet Thomas Green Fessenden on Hancock Street in Beacon Hill in Boston. He was offered an appointment as weigher and gauger at the Boston Custom House at a salary of $1,500 a year, which he accepted on January 17, 1839. During his time there, he rented a room from George Stillman Hillard, business partner of Charles Sumner. Hawthorne wrote in the comparative obscurity of what he called his "owl's nest" in the family home. As he looked back on this period of his life, he wrote: "I have not lived, but only dreamed about living." He contributed short stories to various magazines and annuals, including "Young Goodman Brown" and "The Minister's Black Veil", though none drew major attention to him. Horatio Bridge offered to cover the risk of collecting these stories in the spring of 1837 into the volume Twice-Told Tales, which made Hawthorne known locally.

Marriage and family

While at Bowdoin, Hawthorne wagered a bottle of Madeira wine with his friend Jonathan Cilley that Cilley would get married before Hawthorne did. By 1836, he had won the bet, but he did not remain a bachelor for life. He had public flirtations with Mary Silsbee and Elizabeth Peabody, then he began pursuing Peabody's sister, illustrator and transcendentalist Sophia Peabody. He joined the transcendentalist Utopian community at Brook Farm in 1841, not because he agreed with the experiment but because it helped him save money to marry Sophia. He paid a $1,000 deposit and was put in charge of shoveling the hill of manure referred to as "the Gold Mine". He left later that year, though his Brook Farm adventure became an inspiration for his novel The Blithedale Romance. Hawthorne married Sophia Peabody on July 9, 1842, at a ceremony in the Peabody parlor on West Street in Boston. The couple moved to The Old Manse in Concord, Massachusetts, where they lived for three years. His neighbor Ralph Waldo Emerson invited him into his social circle, but Hawthorne was almost pathologically shy and stayed silent at gatherings. At the Old Manse, Hawthorne wrote most of the tales collected in Mosses from an Old Manse.

Like Hawthorne, Sophia was a reclusive person. Throughout her early life, she had frequent migraines and underwent several experimental medical treatments. She was mostly bedridden until her sister introduced her to Hawthorne, after which her headaches seem to have abated. The Hawthornes enjoyed a long and happy marriage. He referred to her as his "Dove" and wrote that she "is, in the strictest sense, my sole companion; and I need no other—there is no vacancy in my mind, any more than in my heart ... Thank God that I suffice for her boundless heart!" Sophia greatly admired her husband's work. She wrote in one of her journals:

> I am always so dazzled and bewildered with the richness, the depth, the ... jewels of beauty in his productions that I am always looking forward to a second reading where I can ponder and muse and fully take in the miraculous wealth of thoughts.

Poet Ellery Channing came to the Old Manse for help on the first anniversary of the Hawthornes' marriage. A local teenager named Martha Hunt had drowned herself in the river and Hawthorne's boat Pond Lily was needed to find her body. Hawthorne helped recover the corpse, which he described as "a spectacle of such perfect horror ... She was the very image of death-agony". The incident later inspired a scene in his novel The Blithedale Romance.

The Hawthornes had three children. Their first was daughter Una, born March 3, 1844; her name was a reference to The Faerie Queene, to the displeasure of family members. Hawthorne wrote to a friend, "I find it a very sober and serious kind of happiness that springs from the birth of a child ... There is no escaping it any longer. I have business on earth now, and must look about me for the means of doing it." In October 1845, the Hawthornes moved to Salem. In 1846, their son Julian was born. Hawthorne wrote to his sister Louisa on June 22, 1846: "A small troglodyte made his appearance here at ten minutes to six o'clock this morning, who claimed to be your nephew." Daughter Rose was born in May 1851, and Hawthorne called her his "autumnal flower".

Middle years

In April 1846, Hawthorne was officially appointed the Surveyor for the District of Salem and Beverly and Inspector of the Revenue for the Port of Salem at an annual salary of $1,200. He had difficulty writing during this period, as he admitted to Longfellow:

> I am trying to resume my pen ... Whenever I sit alone, or walk alone, I find myself dreaming about stories, as of old; but these forenoons in the Custom House undo all that the afternoons and evenings have done. I should be happier if I could write.

This employment, like his earlier appointment to the custom house in Boston, was vulnerable to the politics of the spoils system. Hawthorne was a Democrat and lost this job due to the change of administration in Washington after the presidential election of 1848. He wrote a letter of protest to the Boston Daily Advertiser which was attacked by the Whigs and supported by the Democrats, making Hawthorne's dismissal a much-talked about event in New England. He was deeply affected by the death of his mother in late July, calling it "the darkest hour I ever lived". He was appointed the corresponding secretary of the Salem Lyceum in 1848. Guests who came to speak that season included Emerson, Thoreau, Louis Agassiz, and Theodore Parker.

Hawthorne returned to writing and published The Scarlet Letter in mid-March 1850, including a preface that refers to his three-year tenure in the Custom House and makes several allusions to local politicians—who did not appreciate their treatment. It was one of the first mass-produced books in America, selling 2,500 volumes within ten days and earning Hawthorne $1,500 over 14 years. The book was pirated by booksellers in London and became a best-seller in the United States; it initiated his most lucrative period as a writer. Hawthorne's friend Edwin Percy Whipple objected to the novel's "morbid intensity" and its dense psychological details, writing that the book "is therefore apt to become, like Hawthorne, too painfully anatomical in his exhibition of them", though 20th-century writer D. H. Lawrence said that there could be no more perfect work of the American imagination than The Scarlet Letter.

Hawthorne and his family moved to a small red farmhouse near Lenox, Massachusetts, at the end of March 1850. He became friends with Herman Melville beginning on August 5, 1850, when the authors met at a picnic hosted by a mutual friend. Melville had just read Hawthorne's short story collection Mosses from an Old Manse, and his unsigned review of the collection was printed in The Literary World on August 17 and August 24 titled "Hawthorne and His Mosses". Melville wrote that these stories revealed a dark side to Hawthorne, "shrouded in blackness, ten times black". He was composing his novel Moby-Dick at the time, and dedicated the work in 1851 to Hawthorne: "In token of my admiration for his genius, this book is inscribed to Nathaniel Hawthorne."

Hawthorne's time in the Berkshires was very productive. While there, he wrote The House of the Seven Gables (1851), which poet and critic James Russell Lowell said was better than The Scarlet Letter and called "the most valuable contribution to New England history that has been made." He also wrote The Blithedale Romance (1852), his only work written in the first person. He also published A Wonder-Book for Girls and Boys in 1851, a collection of short stories retelling myths which he had been thinking about writing since 1846. Nevertheless, poet Ellery Channing reported that Hawthorne "has suffered much living in this place". The family enjoyed the scenery of the Berkshires, although Hawthorne did not enjoy the winters in their small house. They left on November 21, 1851. Hawthorne noted, "I am sick to death of Berkshire ... I have felt languid and dispirited, during almost my whole residence."

The Wayside and Europe

In May 1852, the Hawthornes returned to Concord where they lived until July 1853. In February, they bought The Hillside, a home previously inhabited by Amos Bronson Alcott and his family, and renamed it The Wayside. Their neighbors in Concord included Emerson and Henry David Thoreau. That year, Hawthorne wrote The Life of Franklin Pierce, the campaign biography of his friend which depicted him as "a man of peaceful pursuits". Horace Mann said, "If he makes out Pierce to be a great man or a brave man, it will be the greatest work of fiction he ever wrote." In the biography, Hawthorne depicts Pierce as a statesman and soldier who had accomplished no great feats because of his need to make "little noise" and so "withdrew into the background". He also left out Pierce's drinking habits, despite rumors of his alcoholism, and emphasized Pierce's belief that slavery could not "be remedied by human contrivances" but would, over time, "vanish like a dream".

With Pierce's election as President, Hawthorne was rewarded in 1853 with the position of United States consul in Liverpool shortly after the publication of Tanglewood Tales. The role was considered the most lucrative foreign service position at the time, described by Hawthorne's wife as "second in dignity to the Embassy in London". His appointment ended in 1857 at the close of the Pierce administration, and the Hawthorne family toured France and Italy. During his time in Italy, the previously clean-shaven Hawthorne grew a bushy mustache.

The family returned to The Wayside in 1860, and that year saw the publication of The Marble Faun, his first new book in seven years. Hawthorne admitted that he had aged considerably, referring to himself as "wrinkled with time and trouble".

Later years and death

At the outset of the American Civil War, Hawthorne traveled with William D. Ticknor to Washington, D.C., where he met Abraham Lincoln and other notable figures. He wrote about his experiences in the essay "Chiefly About War Matters" in 1862.

Failing health prevented him from completing several more romance novels. Hawthorne was suffering from pain in his stomach and insisted on a recuperative trip with his friend Franklin Pierce, though his neighbor Bronson Alcott was concerned that Hawthorne was too ill. While on a tour of the White Mountains, he died in his sleep on May 19, 1864, in Plymouth, New Hampshire. Pierce sent a telegram to Elizabeth Peabody asking her to inform Mrs. Hawthorne in person. Mrs. Hawthorne was too saddened by the news to handle the funeral arrangements herself. Hawthorne's son Julian was a freshman at Harvard College, and he learned of his father's death the next day; coincidentally, he was initiated into the Delta Kappa Epsilon fraternity on the same day by being blindfolded and placed in a coffin.Longfellow wrote a tribute poem to Hawthorne published in 1866 called "The Bells of Lynn". Hawthorne was buried on what is now known as "Authors' Ridge" in Sleepy Hollow Cemetery, Concord, Massachusetts. Pallbearers included Longfellow, Emerson, Alcott, Oliver Wendell Holmes Sr., James Thomas Fields, and Edwin Percy Whipple. Emerson wrote of the funeral: "I thought there was a tragic element in the event, that might be more fully rendered—in the painful solitude of the man, which, I suppose, could no longer be endured, & he died of it."

His wife Sophia and daughter Una were originally buried in England. However, in June 2006, they were reinterred in plots adjacent to Hawthorne.

Writings

Hawthorne had a particularly close relationship with his publishers William Ticknor and James Thomas Fields. Hawthorne once told Fields, "I care more for your good opinion than for that of a host of critics." In fact, it was Fields who convinced Hawthorne to turn The Scarlet Letter into a novel rather than a short story. Ticknor handled many of Hawthorne's personal matters, including the purchase of cigars, overseeing financial accounts, and even purchasing clothes. Ticknor died with Hawthorne at his side in Philadelphia in 1864; according to a friend, Hawthorne was left "apparently dazed".

Literary style and themes

Hawthorne's works belong to romanticism or, more specifically, dark romanticism, cautionary tales that suggest that guilt, sin, and evil are the most inherent natural qualities of humanity. Many of his works are inspired by Puritan New England, combining historical romance loaded with symbolism and deep psychological themes, bordering on surrealism. His depictions of the past are a version of historical fiction used only as a vehicle to express common themes of ancestral sin, guilt and retribution. His later writings also reflect his negative view of the Transcendentalism movement.

Hawthorne was predominantly a short story writer in his early career. Upon publishing Twice-Told Tales, however, he noted, "I do not think much of them," and he expected little response from the public. His four major romances were written between 1850 and 1860: The Scarlet Letter (1850), The House of the Seven Gables (1851), The Blithedale Romance (1852) and The Marble Faun (1860). Another novel-length romance, Fanshawe, was published anonymously in 1828. Hawthorne defined a romance as being radically different from a novel by not being concerned with the possible or probable course of ordinary experience. In the preface to The House of the Seven Gables, Hawthorne describes his romance-writing as using "atmospherical medium as to bring out or mellow the lights and deepen and enrich the shadows of the picture". The picture, Daniel Hoffman found, was one of "the primitive energies of fecundity and creation."

Critics have applied feminist perspectives and historicist approaches to Hawthorne's depictions of women. Feminist scholars are interested particularly in Hester Prynne: they recognize that while she herself could not be the "destined prophetess" of the future, the "angel and apostle of the coming revelation" must nevertheless "be a woman." Camille Paglia saw Hester as mystical, "a wandering goddess still bearing the mark of her Asiatic origins ... moving serenely in the magic circle of her sexual nature". Lauren Berlant termed Hester "the citizen as woman [personifying] love as a quality of the body that contains the purest light of nature," her resulting "traitorous political theory" a "Female Symbolic" literalization of futile Puritan metaphors. Historicists view Hester as a protofeminist and avatar of the self-reliance and responsibility that led to women's suffrage and reproductive emancipation. Anthony Splendora found her literary genealogy among other archetypally fallen but redeemed women, both historic and mythic. As examples, he offers Psyche of ancient legend; Heloise of twelfth-century France's tragedy involving world-renowned philosopher Peter Abelard; Anne Hutchinson (America's first heretic, circa 1636), and Hawthorne family friend Margaret Fuller. In Hester's first appearance, Hawthorne likens her, "infant at her bosom", to Mary, Mother of Jesus, "the image of Divine Maternity". In her study of Victorian literature, in which such "galvanic outcasts" as Hester feature prominently, Nina Auerbach went so far as to name Hester's fall and subsequent redemption, "the novel's one unequivocally religious activity". Regarding Hester as a deity figure, Meredith A. Powers found in Hester's characterization "the earliest in American fiction that the archetypal Goddess appears quite graphically," like a Goddess "not the wife of traditional marriage, permanently subject to a male overlord"; Powers noted "her syncretism, her flexibility, her inherent ability to alter and so avoid the defeat of secondary status in a goal-oriented civilization".

Aside from Hester Prynne, the model women of Hawthorne's other novels—from Ellen Langton of Fanshawe to Zenobia and Priscilla of The Blithedale Romance, Hilda and Miriam of The Marble Faun and Phoebe and Hepzibah of The House of the Seven Gables—are more fully realized than his male characters, who merely orbit them. This observation is equally true of his short-stories, in which central females serve as allegorical figures: Rappaccini's beautiful but life-altering, garden-bound, daughter; almost-perfect Georgiana of "The Birthmark"; the sinned-against (abandoned) Ester of "Ethan Brand"; and goodwife Faith Brown, linchpin of Young Goodman Brown's very belief in God. "My Faith is gone!" Brown exclaims in despair upon seeing his wife at the Witches' Sabbath. Perhaps the most sweeping statement of Hawthorne's impetus comes from Mark Van Doren: "Somewhere, if not in the New England of his time, Hawthorne unearthed the image of a goddess supreme in beauty and power."

Hawthorne also wrote nonfiction. In 2008, the Library of America selected Hawthorne's "A show of wax-figures" for inclusion in its two-century retrospective of American True Crime.

96

Criticism

In "Hawthorne and His Mosses", Herman Melville wrote a passionate argument for Hawthorne to be among the burgeoning American literary canon, "He is one of the new, and far better generation of your writers." In this review of Mosses from an Old Manse, Melville describes an affinity for Hawthorne that would only increase: "I feel that this Hawthorne has dropped germinous seeds into my soul. He expands and deepens down, the more I contemplate him; and further, and further, shoots his strong New-England roots into the hot soil of my Southern soul." Edgar Allan Poe wrote important reviews of both Twice-Told Tales and Mosses from an Old Manse. Poe's assessment was partly informed by his contempt of allegory and moral tales, and his chronic accusations of plagiarism, though he admitted,

> The style of Mr. Hawthorne is purity itself. His tone is singularly effective—wild, plaintive, thoughtful, and in full accordance with his themes ... We look upon him as one of the few men of indisputable genius to whom our country has as yet given birth.

Ralph Waldo Emerson wrote, "Nathaniel Hawthorne's reputation as a writer is a very pleasing fact, because his writing is not good for anything, and this is a tribute to the man." Henry James praised Hawthorne, saying, "The fine thing in Hawthorne is that he cared for the deeper psychology, and that, in his way, he tried to become familiar with it." Poet John Greenleaf Whittier wrote that he admired the "weird and subtle beauty" in Hawthorne's tales. Evert Augustus Duyckinck said of Hawthorne, "Of the American writers destined to live, he is the most original, the one least indebted to foreign models or literary precedents of any kind."

Contemporary response to Hawthorne's work praised his sentimentality and moral purity while more modern evaluations focus on the dark psychological complexity. Beginning in the 1950s, critics have focused on symbolism and didacticism.

The critic Harold Bloom opined that only Henry James and William Faulkner challenge Hawthorne's position as the greatest American novelist, although he admitted that he favored James as the greatest American novelist.

Bloom saw Hawthorne's greatest works to be principally The Scarlet Letter, followed by The Marble Faun and certain short stories, including "My Kinsman, Major Molineux", "Young Goodman Brown", "Wakefield", and "Feathertop". (Source: Wikipedia)

NOTABLE WORKS

NOVELS

Fanshawe (published anonymously, 1828)

The Scarlet Letter (1850)

The House of the Seven Gables (1851)

The Blithedale Romance (1852)

The Marble Faun: Or, The Romance of Monte Beni (1860) (as Transformation: Or, The Romance of Monte Beni, UK publication, same year)

The Dolliver Romance (1863) (unfinished)

Septimius Felton; or, the Elixir of Life (unfinished, published in the Atlantic Monthly, 1872)

Doctor Grimshawe's Secret: A Romance (unfinished, with preface and notes by Julian Hawthorne, 1882)

SHORT STORY COLLECTIONS

Twice-Told Tales (1837)

Grandfather's Chair (1840)

Mosses from an Old Manse (1846)

A Wonder-Book for Girls and Boys (1851)

The Snow-Image, and Other Twice-Told Tales (1852)

Tanglewood Tales (1853)

The Dolliver Romance and Other Pieces (1876)

The Great Stone Face and Other Tales of the White Mountains (1889)

SELECTED SHORT STORIES

"The Hollow of the Three Hills" (1830)

"Roger Malvin's Burial" (1832)

"My Kinsman, Major Molineux" (1832)

"The Minister's Black Veil" (1832)

"Young Goodman Brown" (1835)

"The Gray Champion" (1835)

"The White Old Maid" (1835)

"Wakefield" (1835)

"The Ambitious Guest" (1835)

"The Man of Adamant" (1837)

"The May-Pole of Merry Mount" (1837)

"The Great Carbuncle" (1837)

"Dr. Heidegger's Experiment" (1837)

"A Virtuoso's Collection" (May 1842)

"The Birth-Mark" (March 1843)

"The Celestial Railroad" (1843)

"Egotism; or, The Bosom-Serpent" (1843)

"Earth's Holocaust" (1844)

"Rappaccini's Daughter" (1844)

"P.'s Correspondence" (1845)

"The Artist of the Beautiful" (1846)

"Fire Worship" (1846)

"Ethan Brand" (1850)

"The Great Stone Face" (1850)

"Feathertop" (1852)

NONFICTION

Twenty Days with Julian & Little Bunny (written 1851, published 1904)

Our Old Home (1863)

Passages from the French and Italian Notebooks (1871)

CPSIA information can be obtained
at www.ICGtesting.com
Printed in the USA
LVHW051806200720
661094LV00015B/576